THE HEIRESS

LAURA BEERS

The Heiress

By: Laura Beers

Text copyright © 2019 by Laura Beers
Cover art copyright © 2019 by Laura Beers
Cover art by Victoria Cooper Art

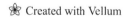 Created with Vellum

MORE ROMANCE FROM LAURA BEERS

The Beckett Files
Regency Spy Romances
Saving Shadow
A Peculiar Courtship
To Love a Spy
A Tangled Ruse
A Deceptive Bargain
The Baron's Daughter
The Unfortunate Debutante

PROLOGUE

Bath, England, 1812

MISS PENELOPE FOSTER NEEDED TO FIND A WAY TO BECOME invisible. Not from everyone, just from the Duke of Blackbourne. Her time at Miss Bell's Finishing School for Young Ladies had come to an end, and she was dreading a missive from the duke.

Five years ago, her parents died, and she had become his ward. A man that she had never met, not once. He had banished her to the finishing school, never sending for her or even communicating with her directly. She had spent the holidays and breaks with Miss Bell rather than her guardian. Or her family. It didn't matter that they had forgotten about her as well, she kept telling herself. She never received one letter from her aunt or cousin, despite her many attempts to reach out to them.

The good news was that Miss Bell had written the duke about her traveling directives, but he didn't bother to respond. Fortunately, Penelope had successfully argued that the Headmistress should allow her to travel to her ancestral home, Brighton Hall, until the duke sent for her. The thought that his grace would force her into a marriage of convenience weighed heavily on her. If she was lucky, he would forget about her entirely... hence her invisibility scheme.

"Dear me," her dear friend, Caroline, broke through her musings. "That is a serious expression. Are you thinking about the Duke of Blackbourne again?" she asked, sitting at a writing table near the window of their dormitory.

Penelope nodded, seeing no reason to deny it. "I am," she said, her eyes meeting the gazes of her concerned friends.

Johana was sitting on her bed, practicing her needlework. "I am not sure why you are fretting. You are an heiress, and not just any heiress. You are the daughter of Sir Foster."

A sad smile came to her lips at the memory of her father. "The duke is my guardian until I marry or turn twenty-one," she reminded them. "He could issue a betrothal contract on my behalf."

"You could become a governess," Adelaide suggested, kneeling beside her trunk. "At least until you are no longer the duke's charge."

"I daresay I am too opinionated to become a governess," Penelope remarked.

Johana let out the most unladylike laugh, lowering the handkerchief in her hand. "So is Adelaide, but she managed to secure a position."

"That's true," Adelaide replied with a forced smile on her lips.

"I am sorry, Adelaide. That was thoughtless on my part." Placing the handkerchief on the bed, Johana rose and went to embrace her. "It will all work out. I promise."

Adelaide turned her attention back towards her trunk as she continued to pack her gowns. "I don't know how. I accepted a governess position in Yorkshire. Whereas, you are all wealthy enough to marry for love, and I will be forced to endure a life-time of servitude."

"You seem to forget that my family's fortune has come from trade," Caroline said with a downcast expression. She rose from her seat and came to sit down next to Penelope on the bed. "We are practically social outcasts. I doubt gentlemen will be lining up to be introduced to me."

"And I refuse to play to the social trappings of society," Johanna declared.

Penelope ran her hand down the length of her Pomona green gown. She had fine gowns, a generous allowance, an estate larger than the whole town near the finishing school, but she didn't have control of her own life. She huffed out a breath of air in frustration. "What a tangled mess we find ourselves in."

Closing the lid of her trunk, Adelaide rose and sat down on the top. "I just hope we will see each other again."

"We will," they answered in unison.

Penelope grimaced, knowing that her situation was similar to Adelaide's, at least until her twenty-first birthday. Until then, she was the duke's charge. His property. He could do with her as he saw fit. It didn't matter that she was an heiress.

She felt unchecked anger starting to build up inside of her. The duke had neglected her and had done nothing to warrant her loyalty. It was time for the Duke of Blackbourne to recognize she would not stand idly by as he attempted to dictate the rest of her life.

"It's time I take control of my own life," she declared suddenly, causing her friends to stare at her. "If I can't be invisible…"

"Invisible?" Caroline asked in confusion.

Penelope smirked. "That was my original plan, but just to the duke."

"I see," Johana remarked, amused. "Invisibility is always a good plan."

3

"As I was saying," she continued, "I will stay at Brighton Hall, and I will refuse to join the dreaded marriage mart."

"What if the duke forces you into a marriage of convenience?" Adelaide asked.

"Then I will run away and hide until my twenty-first birthday," she replied. "I have enough money saved until I could find a governess position or become a companion."

Penelope jumped up from her bed. "I will only marry for love or nothing at all," she exclaimed, eliciting cheers from her friends.

It was time for her to fight for her own happiness. Duke, or no duke... she was no one's property.

ONE MONTH LATER

Nicholas, the Duke of Blackbourne, was having a dreadful day. Correction; he was having a truly, horrific month. And it was only getting worse as he listened to his solicitor ramble on about his vast holdings and the responsibilities that came along with his new title.

His eyes drifted towards the window, and he could see the sea glistening in the distance, inviting him back home. He had been content serving as a captain in His Majesty's Royal Navy. That was, until his father died, making him the eighth Duke of Blackbourne. It was a title that he had never aspired to.

His balding solicitor's next comment broke him out of his stupor of grumbling. "Your mother, the Duchess of Blackbourne, is residing at Hereford Hall, and she expects you to join her for the Season."

"I will not be traveling to London for the Season," Nicholas said frankly, tearing his gaze away from the window.

Mr. Fulton's jaw dropped, emphasizing his double chin. "You must. You are expected in your seat at Parliament."

Nicholas leaned forward in his chair and placed his forearms on the desk. "I have been at sea for the past eight years. I daresay that I am not well-enough informed on the issues to vote at this time."

"Your father was a Tory, as was your uncle, but you are not required to pick a political party, assuming that is your concern."

"My views align with the Tories, but that is not the issue," he shared. "Lawrence Abbey needs my full attention."

Mr. Fulton waved his hand dismissively. "That is why you have a steward. Leave it in his capable hands and travel to London."

"I prefer to be more involved with my investments," he replied, growing more irritated by the minute.

"You won't have time anymore. You have much more pressing issues," Mr. Fulton contended. "Besides, you have three other estates that you could reside in, not including your London townhouse. Why did you pick the most dilapidated estate, and in the town of Swansea, of all places?"

Nicholas adopted his sternest glare and aimed it at his impertinent solicitor. "Lawrence Abbey is where I was raised, and I believe our copper smelters are underperforming." That was the partial truth. He had loved spending his youth riding along the coast with his brother and exploring the ruins in the hills surrounding his estate. He felt his countenance dimming as he thought of his brother. How he missed him!

"But, sir, your copper smelters are only a small percentage of your wealth. As the Duke of Blackbourne, it is of paramount importance that you assume your proper place in society."

"I do not like to be told what to do, and I tire of your useless chatter. I would like to adjourn this meeting to deal with more pressing issues." Nicholas lifted his brow. "Unless there is any other pertinent information that I need to be made aware of?"

Looking contrite, Mr. Fulton reached for a file and opened it up. "My humblest apologies, your grace." He pulled out a paper and held it up. "The last issue we need to discuss is what you plan to do with your ward now that she has finished with Miss Bell's Finishing School for Young Ladies."

"*My what*?!"

Seeming unperturbed by his sudden outburst, Mr. Fulton informed him, "Miss Penelope Foster was your uncle's ward, then briefly became your father's ward when he inherited the title, and now she is your responsibility. At least until she gets married or turns twenty-one."

Nicholas brought his fingers up to the bridge of his nose and took a deep breath to calm his nerves. This could not be happening to him.

"When exactly did my uncle obtain a ward?"

"Five years ago."

He was attempting to make sense of this new information. "Is she a poor relation?"

Mr. Fulton chuckled, drawing his attention back up to him. "No, your grace. She is the only child of Sir Charles and Lady Edith Foster, who were dear friends of your Uncle Alfred. He served as one of Miss Foster's godfathers."

"Does this Miss Foster have no other family to speak of?"

Adjusting his brown jacket, Mr. Fulton frowned. "That is a debatable issue. Your uncle did not trust Miss Foster's relations and discouraged any contact with them."

"Why?"

"Miss Foster's uncle, Lord Mountgarret, was a known gambler and lacked scruples, by all accounts," his solicitor explained. "Your uncle ordered me to send Miss Foster off to finishing school, under the strictest confidence, and to keep her whereabouts unknown."

Nicholas furrowed his brow. "Why the secrecy?"

Mr. Fulton glanced over his shoulder, then leaned a little closer. "Miss Foster is the sole heir of the Foster Company. It is roughly valued at one hundred million pounds."

"She is an heiress."

"Yes, many times over. Furthermore, her father dealt on the London stock exchange in financial instruments such as foreign bills and government securities," his solicitor went on, sitting up straight again. "Your ward is immensely wealthy and needs to be protected from fortune hunters."

"Blazes," he mumbled under his breath. What was he going to do with a ward that was also an heiress? "Does this Miss Foster know the full extent of her expansive fortune?"

Mr. Fulton shook his head. "Her parents died when she was twelve, and she was sent off to the finishing school immediately thereafter. Your uncle requested that she not be told of her full inheritance at her tender age."

Poor girl, he thought. His uncle had just cast her aside. "Why didn't my uncle have her come live with him and hire a governess?"

"At the time, he was newly married and was not prepared to take in a ward," his solicitor stated.

"So, he sent her off to be raised by others?" Nicholas asked, his voice rising in indignation.

"He did what he thought was best for the girl," Mr. Fulton explained. "Her paternal aunt, Lady Diana, wife of Lord Mount-garret, did petition Parliament for custody but was rejected."

"Did she state why she should gain custody?"

"She claimed that her brother's will was outdated, and that she should maintain custody over her niece."

Nicholas leaned back in his seat. "I take it that Parliament rejected her plea."

"Aye, your grace. Lady Diana was furious and left in a huff," Mr. Fulton shared.

"Did Parliament state a reason for the rejection?"

His solicitor nodded. "Your uncle successfully argued that Lord Mountgarret would take advantage of Miss Penelope Foster's wealth as her guardian, especially since he had already gambled away his family's fortune."

"Was Sir Foster estranged from his sister?"

Mr. Fulton reached for another paper in the file. "Not at all. In fact, their estates bordered each other's near Cardiff, and they were often spotted socializing during the Season in London." He extended it across the desk. "Lady Diana had been estranged from her husband for almost two decades before he passed away two years ago."

"Did they have any children?"

"Just one. Her son, Lord Mountgarret, is an active member of the Tory party, and studied to be a barrister at Oxford."

Nicholas finally took a moment to peruse the paper in his hand. "What is this list?" he asked, turning the paper over and seeing more writing.

"Those are the balls, soirees, house parties, and events which you will be expected to attend, alongside your charge, this Season," Mr. Fulton replied.

He dropped the paper to the desk. "This list is unfathomably long."

His solicitor appeared unphased by his complaint as he continued. "Miss Penelope Foster has been living at the finishing school for the past five years. She just turned eighteen, and it is time for her to be introduced into society."

Nicholas stifled a groan. His infuriating solicitor was right. "Do you suppose my mother would introduce her into society?"

Mr. Fulton gave him a curt nod. "Your father has been deceased for a little over a year, so your mother may be in half-mourning now. I have no doubt she would help you with this precarious situation."

"Did my father show any interest in Miss Foster?" he asked, bringing his hand up to his chin.

His solicitor frowned. "After I informed him of Miss Foster and her whereabouts, he insisted that she remain at the finishing school. He was planning on marrying her off at his earliest convenience, and no doubt he would have profited from the deal."

Sadly, that did not surprise him. His father was not known for his kindness. "Where exactly is my ward?"

"Last month, she returned to her family's ancestral estate, Brighton Hall, in Cardiff."

"Why was I not informed earlier of my ward and her location?" he asked, rising from his seat.

Mr. Fulton reached over and collected a paper that had dropped to the ground. "You were a difficult man to track down. Your father died more than a year ago, but you failed to respond to any of my missives in the months thereafter. With no choice, I appealed to the Navy Board, but it still took almost three months to locate you at sea and another month for you to travel home. Even after you finally arrived on British soil three weeks ago, it still took me two weeks to track you down."

"We are at war, or did you forget that detail, Mr. Fulton?" Nicholas asked with irritation in his voice. "My loyalty is to my King and country." He pointed towards the window. "I was fighting to keep the channel safe from our enemies, which is much more important than being in full dress, masquerading at balls with the frivolous members of the ton."

His solicitor swallowed slowly. "My apologies, your grace."

Nicholas walked over to the drink tray and poured himself a brandy, ignoring his solicitor's weak apology. "Do we know if Lady Diana has attempted to make contact with Miss Foster now that she has returned home?"

"Lady Diana is deceased," his solicitor informed him.

"Excellent." He took a sip of his drink, knowing his words were callous. It was one less complication that he would have to deal with. "I would like you to personally escort my ward to my mother in London. I will travel to town at my earliest convenience."

Mr. Fulton rose from his seat and bowed. "As you wish, your

grace."

Nicholas didn't feel the need to say anything else as he watched his solicitor organize all the papers into a file. He turned his gaze out the window and watched the waves lap lazily along the shores of the Gower Peninsula. How his heart longed to be back at sea. To be the captain of his ship again. Instead, he was a duke, and somehow, he'd inherited a ward. A blasted eighteen-year-old girl.

Well, his mother would see to the girl, and he would ensure that fortune hunters steered clear of her. He brought the glass to his lips as he considered the optimal course of action for Miss Foster. She needed to marry a respectable man. With any luck, he would have her married off by the end of the Season.

He placed his glass on the tray and sighed. He didn't know much about debutantes, but how much trouble could they possibly pose?

Penelope raced her horse through the fields near Brighton Hall. Her dark brown hair flowed scandalously behind her as she closed her eyes, feeling the wind hitting her face. A feeling of peace washed over her as she recognized that no one dictated her every move here. She was free. It was a miraculous feeling.

She slowed her horse's gait as she approached the woodlands near the edge of her property. She heard, rather than saw, the two footmen trailing behind her.

Her horse stepped onto a small worn path through the trees, and she was immediately cloaked in green shade. Birds chirped in the trees, squirrels scurried away as she rode passed, and a group of deer continued to eat the shrubbery, staring at her while chewing. This was her haven. She continued down the path until her horse stopped to take a drink at a large pond with lily pads dotting the surface.

After dismounting, Penelope removed her straw bonnet and held it to her side as she lifted her face up towards the heavens. It had been one month since she had left the finishing school. She had been lucky enough to make some dear, lifelong friends, but her heart still mourned the loss of her parents.

"Cousin," a familiar voice said from the other side of the pond. "What a lovely day to go for a ride, is it not?"

"It is," she acknowledged.

"May I join you on your side of the pond?" he asked merrily.

She let out an exasperated sigh as if she was being put out. "I suppose so."

Her cousin, Baldwin Ellis, the Viscount of Mountgarret, laughed as he veered his horse towards a section of the pond that could be easily waded through. She took a moment to acknowledge that they shared similar features with their dark brown hair, narrow noses, and tall, thin frames. Besides being handsome, her cousin had an easy smile and a charismatic personality.

The pond was the physical barrier between her land and her cousin's. When she had first arrived home, she had been informed that she was not allowed to step foot on Lord Mountgarret's land, for any reason. Her butler explained that it was a long-standing order from the Duke of Blackbourne, and she didn't dare disobey, for he had the power to move her to another estate far away from Brighton Hall. Rather than disobey the command, she found a way around it. The duke hadn't specifically issued a command about seeing her cousin, so they would meet frequently at the pond.

Once Baldwin was on her side, he dismounted and walked his horse over to hers. "Are you alone?" he asked, his eyes scanning the trees.

"Of course not," she replied as the two footmen made their presence known. She smiled over at them and waved.

"Excellent," her cousin said. "Your reputation is the— "

"Most important thing that I have. I remember," she stated, cutting him off.

Baldwin chuckled. "What have you done today?"

Penelope reached down, picked a red flower, and brought it to her nose. "I visited the vicar and his chatty wife this morning and brought food to a woman that had just given birth. Later, I met with my steward and he started explaining to me about how to run an estate…"

Baldwin spoke over her. "That's not necessary. You are just a woman and can't possibly understand the nuances of running an estate."

"How primeval of you," she remarked lightly.

He laughed, as she hoped he would. "If you require any assistance, I would be happy to help you."

"I know." Her horse pawed at the ground. "But I want to learn. It is important to me."

Reaching out, Baldwin rubbed her horse's neck and said, "Then it is important to me."

"Thank you, Cousin," she murmured, turning her gaze back towards the pond.

"Have you received correspondence from the Duke of Black-bourne yet?"

She brought her gaze back towards his. "Not yet. His grace has not requested my presence for the Season. For which I am grateful. I don't want to rush into the marriage mart."

"I should hope not."

Penelope pressed her lips together, considering her next words carefully. "Were you visiting your mother's grave again?"

He nodded, reflectively.

"Do you know why I was kept from your family all these years?"

Baldwin turned his gaze towards the pond and didn't speak for a long moment. "I don't know all the reasons, but I must assume it was because of my father's rubbish reputation." He brought his gaze back to hers. "But know this, my mother fought valiantly to obtain custody of you. She loved you like her own daughter."

"I wish I had been able to see her one last time."

"As did she." Baldwin smiled fondly at her. "Remember, I will be gone for the Season since I am expected at Parliament, but I will look forward to seeing you when I retire to my country home."

"Perhaps you will be married by the end of the Season?" she teased.

He stiffened. "There is little chance of that."

That was a peculiar reaction to her remark, she observed.

"Well, I can't wait to hear of your stories and triumphs in Parliament," she said, changing the subject.

"Miss Foster," a footman announced, breaking through the trees. "A Mr. Fulton is here to call upon you."

Baldwin eyed her suspiciously. "Who exactly is Mr. Fulton?"

"He is the duke's solicitor."

Penelope attempted to hide her apprehension as she walked over to the left side of her horse.

"Allow me." Baldwin clasped his hands low, so she could mount her side saddle. "Would you like me to come with you?"

"No, thank you," she replied, adjusting her skirts.

He bowed. "Then I shall see you after the conclusion of the Season."

"I am looking forward to it," she responded, smiling.

Turning her horse towards the trail, she maneuvered out of the woodland area and raced her horse through the fields until Brighton Hall loomed ahead. It was a Gothic medieval castle that her father had restored before her birth. With its majestic turrets, narrow windows, towers jutting up on both ends of the four-level structure, and underground grotto, it was truly a magnificent place to call home.

A black closed carriage with the Duke of Blackbourne's emblem sat in her courtyard and was being watched over by her footmen. She reined in her horse and slid off with expert precision.

"Thank you," Penelope murmured as she extended her reins towards a groomsman.

As she walked up the stairs, the door was opened and her aging butler, Mr. Watts, tilted his head respectfully.

"Mr. Fulton is waiting for you in the drawing room."

"Did he state his business?" she asked, removing her riding gloves.

"No, Miss, but I did order refreshments to be sent up," he informed her, holding out his hand for her gloves.

She smiled gratefully at him. "Thank you for seeing to that. You have been a god-send to me since I returned home."

"It's my pleasure," Mr. Watts replied with kindness in his tone. "We have missed you these past five years, and we are glad you're home where you belong."

"It is nice to be home."

Penelope proceeded towards the drawing room and was greeted by Mr. Fulton the moment she entered the room.

"Good morning, Miss Foster," he said with a bow.

"Good morning, Mr. Fulton."

Standing by the window, the light reflected off his bald head as he expressed, "I am glad that you remember me. It has been a few years since we last spoke."

"Five, to be exact," Penelope stated more forcefully than she intended.

"Yes... well, that was per the Duke of Blackbourne's wishes."

"May I ask why?" she asked, gracefully lowering herself onto a camelback settee.

He cleared his throat nervously. "You must know that your parents were wealthy and left you a great sum of money."

Penelope pressed her lips together to refrain from the scathing retort she had intended to say. Once she had composed herself, she replied, "How would I have known that? While I knew of my wealth by my upbringing, the extent of it was never told to me. I was sent off to Miss Bell's Finishing School for Young Ladies the day after my parents were buried. I spent my holidays at the school, and I did not receive one letter from you or from the duke in all my years there."

"It was in your best interest..."

She placed her hand up, eager to end this futile conversation. "Are you here to discuss my finances?"

Mr. Fulton adjusted his waistcoat as he answered, "No. You have a team of men that are managing your investments and interests. It would be much too complicated for a woman as young as yourself to understand the intricacies of your vast holdings."

"I see," she replied disappointedly. "Then I must assume you are here on behalf of his grace."

Mr. Fulton stepped away from the window and came to sit across from her. "You may not have heard, but the Duke of Blackbourne died two years ago after contracting influenza. His brother then inherited the title but died suddenly last year. His son, Nicholas, is now the eighth Duke of Blackbourne, and he has requested your presence in London for the upcoming Season."

Dread washed over her. The duke did intend to marry her off, so she would no longer be his ward.

"I have been instructed to escort you to London where you will be introduced into society by his grace's mother, the Duchess of Blackbourne," he explained, seeming oblivious to her shock. "Once your trunks have been packed, we can depart."

Penelope stood quickly, causing Mr. Fulton to rise awkwardly. "Please inform his grace that I am not interested in going to London for the Season."

"You must," Mr. Fulton stated. "The duke has ordered it, and you are his ward."

"What exactly does that mean, Mr. Fulton?" she questioned in anger. "The Duke of Blackbourne was not only my guardian, but he was my godfather as well. However, he never once visited me or showed me favor of any kind. I was a burden to him."

Mr. Fulton shook his head profusely. "You have it all wrong…"

She tilted her chin defiantly. "I wasn't even informed of his passing, or that I was handed down to each subsequent Duke of Blackbourne thereafter."

"That was poorly done, I admit," he said, having the decency to look embarrassed.

Penelope stood her ground, but she softened her tone. "I apologize for putting you in an awkward situation, I truly am. But I have no wish to be a burden any longer, and I am content living my days in Cardiff. Please inform the duke of my decision."

"His grace is not a man to be trifled with, miss," he warned.

"Good. Perhaps he might feel a smidgeon of what I felt when I was abandoned at that finishing school."

A fleeting look of trepidation passed over the solicitor's face. It was obvious that he feared the duke. "I must again advise you not to anger his grace."

She clasped her hands in front of her. "If he is anything like his predecessors, he will be relieved to know that I wish to be left alone. One less burden for him to concern himself with."

"I assure you that he is nothing like the previous dukes."

"Then I will look forward to meeting him one day," she proclaimed. "Good day, sir."

Penelope spun around and strode out of the room without looking back. She refused to defer to any man… including the new Duke of Blackbourne.

❦ 2 ❦

NICHOLAS PLACED THE QUILL NEXT TO THE INKPOT AS HIS EYES scanned over his mahogany desk. He needed to hire a secretary, and quickly. Mr. Fulton had given him six large stacks of letters, each tied with a bulging string, and informed him that it was crucial to stay on top of his correspondences. Life had been much simpler on his ship. He logged daily in a captain's log, assembled daily meetings with his lieutenants, and ensured that everything was up to snuff. Everything was done in precisely the same manner. Every. Day. It was predictable. It was perfect.

Even their attacks on other ships were planned down to the last variable. His crew had been trained to expect the unexpected, and he pushed them to be better through their rigorous training sessions. He never asked his crew to do something that he wasn't willing to do, and he fought alongside them. His crew became his family.

"I know that look," came a familiar voice from across the room. "You are debating about running back to your ship."

Nicholas turned his gaze towards the door and saw his friend, Everett, the Marquess of Northampton, standing in the doorway.

"I am," he admitted, rising from his seat. "If I have to sign my name on one more document, I fear that I might literally go mad."

Everett laughed. "You are a duke, and I can't even imagine the number of correspondences that you must receive. I am only a humble marquess."

"You were raised knowing that you would inherit your title," Nicholas pointed out, walking over to his drink cart, "whereas I was never supposed to be the duke."

"It is a shame that so many members of your family have passed away."

He took the lid off the decanter as he replied. "My uncle's first wife, Victoria, had no problem bearing children, but they never lived past infancy." He poured the brandy into two glasses. "After her death, he married a woman forty years his junior, and I had high hopes that she would beget him a son. Unfortunately, my uncle died from influenza before that happened, bringing the line of succession to my father."

Everett looked at him with amusement. "Cheer up, my friend. You have inherited a dukedom, not the plague."

"I already acquired wealth and status, and I commanded my own frigate. I never aspired to be a duke," he shared, walking over and extending the glass to his friend.

Reaching out, Everett accepted the drink from him. "Take heart in knowing you are not alone. You have been given a great responsibility, and I believe you will rise to the challenge."

Nicholas let out a grunt. "You have always been too optimistic for my taste." He tossed back his drink. "Why are you here bothering me?"

Grinning, Everett brought the glass up to his lips. "Your mother sent me."

"My mother?"

His friend sat down on an upholstered settee. "Yes. She is concerned that you won't travel to London for the Season."

"That had been my initial plan but…" he hesitated, "my plans have since changed."

Everett watched him with a curious expression. "Have they now?"

"Your grace," his butler spoke up from the doorway. "Mr. Fulton is here to see you. He says his business is most urgent."

"Mr. Fulton is here?" he asked through gritted teeth. His solicitor was supposed to be traveling to London with his ward. What was he doing here? "Send him in."

Nicholas placed his empty glass onto his desk and waited for his incompetent solicitor to explain what the blazes was going on.

Mr. Fulton walked into the room, wringing his hat in front of him. "Your grace," he acknowledged. "I went to inform Miss Foster of your wishes and to escort her to London, but she…" His voice trailed off as he lowered his gaze.

"She what?" he demanded.

Mr. Fulton brought his gaze up. "She declined."

"What?" he replied in a steely tone. "She can't decline my direct order."

Pursing his lips, his solicitor explained, "Miss Foster stated that she has no desire to go to London for the Season. Furthermore, she requests that you leave her be in Cardiff."

He clenched his jaw. "Did she state a reason?"

"Miss Foster expressed some resentment at your uncle's decision to send her off to the finishing school and leaving her there for the past five years," his solicitor said.

"Did my uncle or father not send for her during the holidays or breaks?" he questioned, fearing he already knew the answer.

Mr. Fulton shook his head. "No, your grace."

No wonder his ward held such resentment! She had been banished, neglected. He knew what needed to be done. He would handle this himself. "I will call on her and escort her to London myself."

A relieved sigh came from Mr. Fulton. "Thank you, your grace." He bowed and departed from the room without another word.

Nicholas understood Miss Foster's reluctant attitude, but he would chastise her for disobeying his orders. When he gave a command, it was to be followed, precisely.

"Who is Miss Foster?" Everett asked.

"My ward."

"*Your what?*"

Nicholas came to sit across from his friend. "Penelope is the daughter of Sir Charles Foster and heir to the Foster Company."

His friend's next words were deliberate. "Your ward is Miss Penelope Foster?"

"Yes."

To his annoyance, Everett leaned back against the sofa and started laughing. "You are one unlucky bloke. I have heard that the Foster fortune is close to nearly a billion pounds."

Nicholas winced. "Now do you see my issue?"

"How do you intend to protect her? Fortune hunters will come out in droves when they hear that she is in London for the Season."

A perfect solution came to his mind. "Would you like to marry her?"

Everett's eyes flashed with disappointment. "You don't intend to marry her off at the first opportunity, do you?"

He let out a loud groan. "Yes… no. I don't know the first thing about being a guardian to an eighteen- year-old girl."

"For starters, you need to call on her," Everett advised, rising from his seat. "Do not neglect her like your predecessors did. She deserves better."

"You're right."

Everett offered him a gloating smile. "Of course I am."

"I will see that my trunks are packed, and then I shall depart for Cardiff. Would you like to join us as we travel to London?"

"I wouldn't miss it for the world," Everett said.

Penelope was in the library when she saw the Duke of Black-bourne's black coach come up over the hill near her estate. Drat! She should have known that Mr. Fulton wouldn't have stayed away for long. He probably scurried back to the duke and was sent back to issue another ridiculous command.

The coach came to a stop in the courtyard, and a hand reached out from the window to open the door. A tall, dark-haired man, with a well-defined nose and chiseled jaw, stepped out of the coach. His muscular frame was evident in his blue riding jacket and buff trousers. The man's dark eyebrows were sloped downward in a stern expression as his eyes swept over Brighton Hall.

Penelope kept watching the handsome man until she saw another attractive man exit the carriage. He had dark blonde hair, was similar height, and had sharp features, but he did not capti-vate her attention like the first man had.

She placed her book on the table and swiftly headed out of the library. These men must be employed by the duke, but she was unsure of their capacity. Stopping at the top of the stairs, she was curious to discover their identities.

A loud knock echoed throughout the entry hall. Mr. Watts opened the door and a smooth, but authoritative, baritone voice declared, "I am the Duke of Blackbourne, and I would like to speak to my ward, Miss Penelope Foster."

"Of course, your grace," Mr. Watts replied, gesturing them inside.

Penelope's eyes widened as she saw the man that had first caught her attention walk into the entry foyer. His steps were full of purpose and authority. That was the Duke of Blackbourne? Good heavens! Dukes were supposed to be old and wrinkly, she thought. Well, this only slightly altered her battle plan.

Penelope ran down the hall and flung open her bedchamber door. "I need to change," she announced, startling her lady's maid.

"Would you like to wear an afternoon dress?" Claire asked, resuming her task of organizing the bedchamber.

"No. I have something better in mind," she replied, strategically pulling out tendrils from her chignon. "Do we still have my mother's orange gown?"

"You cannot be serious? That dress was hideous, even for six years ago." Claire looked at her with a baffled expression. "What are you doing to your hair?"

"My guardian, the Duke of Blackbourne, has come to call, and I need to convince him that I am not suitable to go to London for the Season," she explained rationally.

"How? By dressing in a costume gown and looking unkept?"

Penelope walked over to the dressing table and opened the top drawer. She rummaged through it until she found what she was looking for: her father's large round spectacles. "No. I need to prove that I am not marriageable material."

"He has eyes," Claire contended. "One look at you, and he will recognize you for the unique beauty that you are."

"That is where these spectacles come in."

Penelope placed them high onto her nose, causing the room to become very blurry. Turning her gaze towards Claire, she saw a woman's shape but could not make out any distinct features. She took them off and looked at them in shock.

"I can barely see anything with these on."

"They weren't designed for you," Claire stated as she draped a gown over her arm. "Do you truly want me to retrieve that orange gown from your mother's closet?"

"It is not packed away in the attic?"

Claire shook her head. "No. All of your mother's clothing is still preserved in her bedchamber."

"Oh," she murmured. "I failed to notice."

"It is understandable, Miss. I imagine it must be hard for you to spend time in your parent's bedchambers," her lady's maid commented.

"It is," she replied, her countenance dimming. It had been over a month since she'd arrived home, but she had yet to spend any substantial time in her parent's bedchambers. It always brought back a flood of memories, leaving her emotionally drained.

A knock came at her door. "Enter," she commanded.

Her housekeeper, Mrs. Cooley, opened the door. "The Duke of Blackbourne is here to see you, Miss," she announced, smiling kindly, as she always did. "You best not keep him waiting long."

Penelope returned her smile. "Please let his grace know I will be down shortly."

"As you wish," she replied before closing the door.

Turning back towards her lady's maid, she ordered, "Please go retrieve that dress, and hurry."

"I hope you know what you are doing," Claire said before departing to do her bidding.

A short time later, Penelope was dressed in an orange high-waisted gown, with white lace framing the neckline and sleeves that gathered near her elbow. Her mother had worn this dress to a costume ball, and she had no doubt that it appeared quite hideous on her. Perfect.

She stopped outside of the drawing room and took a deep breath. It was time for her to play a role, a role that would set her free. Placing the spectacles onto her face, she walked into the room and noticed two blurry men standing near the fireplace.

Penelope placed her hands out in front of her and walked until she bumped into the back of the camelback sofa. "I apologize for keeping you waiting, but it takes some time for me to move around," she informed them in a meek voice.

"You are Miss Penelope Foster, I presume," a man's voice asked.

She directed her gaze towards him. "I am. And you are?"

"I am Nicholas, the Duke of Blackbourne," he cleared his throat, "and apparently your guardian."

A smile came to her face, causing her spectacles to shift. She brought her left hand back up to adjust them. "It is a pleasure to meet you, your grace."

He walked towards her, and she could make out a few of his features, albeit blurry. "My solicitor failed to inform me of your… condition."

"My condition?" she repeated, pretending to feign ignorance.

"Pardon me, where are my manners," the duke said. "Allow me to introduce my good friend, Everett Beauchamp, the Marquess of Northampton."

The other blurry outline spoke. "It is a pleasure to meet you, Miss Foster."

"The pleasure is all mine, Lord Northampton." She pointed towards the chairs. "Please be seated. I have requested refreshment to be served."

Taking her hand, she glided it along the back of the sofa until she came around the front and was able to sit down. "Your grace, I apologize for sending Mr. Fulton away, but I do not feel comfortable leaving Brighton Hall at this time."

"I understand," he said from his seated position. "Are you being well taken care of here?"

"Oh yes," she gushed. "I get to wear these pretty gowns, and the staff is kind to me."

An awkward silence filled the room, and she felt no need to speak up. This was going splendidly. She saw the duke glance over at his friend. No words were exchanged, but she had no doubt an unspoken understanding passed between them.

His grace spoke up. "I will speak to your steward and ensure that you have enough funds at your disposal."

She tucked a piece of hair behind her ear. "There is no need. Mr. Albott has been gracious enough to explain the basics of my allowance."

"I see," came the duke's voice. "How bad is your vision, if I may ask?"

"Limited. I require the use of these spectacles to see," she lied, pushing them up against her nose.

"I will send for a specialist to examine your eyes," Nicholas informed her. "Perhaps there might be something done to help your vision."

Penelope found herself speechless by his show of compassion. She had not expected that. For the first time, she felt a twinge of guilt for lying to him.

"That is most kind of you," she murmured.

"Is there anything that you need that I can assist you with?" the duke asked.

She shook her head. "I am content here at Brighton Hall, but I thank you."

Rising, his grace inquired, "Thank you for meeting with me, Miss Foster. I will start sending weekly correspondences and... um... will you be able to read them?"

She rose, keeping her hand firmly on her spectacles. "Yes, if I press the letter close enough to my face."

"Very good then," the duke said as Lord Northampton came to stand next to him.

A knock came at the main entry door, followed by the very loud, boisterous voice of Mrs. Ashton. Penelope's heart dropped. That busy-body would ruin everything!

"It appears that the vicar's wife has come to call," she rushed out. "Thank you for taking the time to stop by, your grace." She turned towards the blurry outline of Lord Northampton. "And it was a pleasure to meet you, Lord Northampton."

The duke took a step closer to her. "If you need anything, please send word and…"

"Good heavens, child," came Mrs. Ashton's squeaky voice. "You look a fright."

Mr. Watt's voice came from the doorway. "Mrs. Ashton is here to see you."

Penelope turned towards the offending noise and replied, "Hello, Mrs. Ashton. I will be with you shortly."

Mrs. Ashton walked closer, and she had no doubt the busy body's nose was squished up in disapproval. "When did you start wearing spectacles?"

The duke's voice came from behind her. "Does Miss Foster not normally wear spectacles?"

"I just saw her this morning racing through her fields on her horse," Mrs. Ashton shared in a disapproving tone. "I often have thought she was going to break her neck at the speeds she rides."

"Is that so?" the duke responded through gritted teeth.

Penelope spoke up. "If you will excuse me…" Her words were stopped when the duke gripped her upper arm, halting her retreat.

"Out of curiosity, does Miss Foster normally dress in this style of clothing?" the duke inquired.

Mrs. Ashton shook her head. "Heavens, no. She is always fashionably dressed even when delivering baskets to members of our parish." She stepped closer and lowered her voice. "Are you well, Miss Foster? Should I call for a doctor?"

She closed her eyes in mortification. "I am well, Mrs. Ashton. I thank you for your concern."

The duke's grip tightened on her arm, but she didn't dare tell him that he was hurting her.

"I need to speak to my ward alone, *now*," the duke declared.

Lord Northampton quickly escorted Mrs. Ashton from the room and only when the door closed did the duke drop his grip from her arm.

"I do not like to be lied to, Miss Foster," he growled with such ferocity that it caused her to jump.

Knowing that her ruse had failed, Penelope removed the spectacles and slid them into her pocket. She slowly turned around and faced a very angry duke.

☙ 3 ❧

NICHOLAS WATCHED HIS WARD TURN AROUND, AND HE SAW A flicker of fear in her eyes. Good. She should be afraid of him. But to his astonishment, it was quickly replaced with determination. He had not expected that.

He had another problem. Penelope was not the young miss that he had envisioned. She was a beautiful woman with brown hair, narrow nose, elegant cheekbones, and wide, expressive blue eyes that would enchant even the weakest fool.

His first responsibility was to ensure that his ward knew her place and understood that he was in charge. "Explain to me why I should not cane you for your deliberate attempt to deceive me?"

"You would not dare," she replied defiantly.

He took a commanding step towards her. "It is within my rights as your guardian."

"My intention was for you to allow me to stay at Brighton Hall by appearing unmarriageable," she explained in a rational tone.

"For what purpose?" he asked, his voice strained.

Rather than cower, or step back, his ward tilted her head to look up at him. "I refuse to go to London and be married off without so much as a say in my life."

"You are an heiress. It would be in your best interest to marry, and quickly."

"I have no intention of marrying this Season," she asserted.

That would not do. If Miss Foster didn't marry this Season, then she would remain his ward for another year. Another burden.

"Regardless, you will go to London for the Season, and my mother will introduce you into society," he said, his tone brooking no argument. Once she got to London, he was positive that she would see reason.

"I will not," came her quick reply.

His eyes narrowed at her impertinence. He had just issued an order. "It was not a request," he grunted.

"I perceived as much."

Insubordination. "You are not in a position to deny my request."

To his surprise, she drew herself up to her full height before saying, "I know exactly what you intend to do with me, your grace," she said in a matter-of-fact tone. "Your plan is to marry me off at your first opportunity, because I am only a burden to you."

Nicholas had to admit that she was a clever, determined thing. However, these were not good qualities for a woman to possess if she ever hoped to marry. "I am not so callous as to marry you off without first discussing it with you."

She arched a perfectly shaped eyebrow. "Why should you, a man that I have never met before now, have control over my future? How is that fair?"

"It's not, but you are a woman," he contended, "and by such, you need the protection of a man."

"Then I will hire guards to ensure my safety."

"That will not be sufficient." Nicholas glared down at her,

but she met his gaze with a fiery intensity. This would not do. He couldn't very well beat the girl into submission. He needed to change tactics. It was time to negotiate. He took a step back and pointed towards the sofa. "Perhaps if we can come to a new understanding."

Penelope eyed him suspiciously. "What do you propose?"

Your surrender, he thought to himself. "Please sit."

"I prefer to stand, your grace," she replied, not wavering in her stance.

Nicholas took his time as he walked over to the window and looked out over the expansive green fields that surrounded Brighton Hall. He meant to intimidate her by taking back control of the conversation.

"Come for the Season, and I will allow you to select your husband, assuming he is a titled gentleman with an impeccable reputation."

"I do not accept your terms."

Clasping his hands behind his back, he turned and asked, "Then what exactly are you looking for in a husband?"

"I will marry for love or not at all," she stated in a straight forward manner.

Her answer caught him off guard. What nonsense had they filled her head with at that finishing school?

"Love is not tangible in our circles. Surely you must know that."

There was no hesitation or doubt in her voice as she replied, "You are wrong. It is completely possible to obtain a love match."

Nicholas curled his lip, trying not to show too much emotion. "You have read too many books. Love only belongs in fairy tales."

He expected a quick retort, but she lowered her gaze and turned away from him. The only sound in the room was the ticking from the floor clock, and the silence became deafening.

She must think of him as an ogre, but it was better for her to know the truth. Love was not possible for people in their positions. She needed to prepare herself for the inevitable marriage of convenience.

Penelope turned back towards him, her movements precise. "I will go to London for the Season, but only if I am allowed to select my own suitor, a man of my own choosing. But, more important, a man that I have fallen in love with."

"Unacceptable," he exclaimed, bringing his arms to his sides. "You are my ward and will not dictate the terms to me."

Penelope's candid gaze unnerved him, and she appeared to be in no rush to respond to his outburst. It was as if she was searching his soul and found him lacking.

"You want to be my guardian no more than I want to be your ward," she started off slowly.

"True, but that…"

She took a step closer and spoke over him. "If you force me to go to London, then I will run away."

"I will find you," he asserted, taking a step closer to her.

"No, you won't, and if you did, I would continue running," she declared. "I only need to hide until my twenty-first birthday, and I have no qualms about finding employment."

He took another step closer to her and was now within a few feet of her. "You would seek employment just to defy me?"

"No. I would seek employment to avoid a marriage that I do not want," she contested.

His ward was good at negotiating, but he was better. "I would lock you up then," he threatened.

"You could," she murmured. "But you won't."

Now he wanted to throttle her. She had called his bluff. He glowered down at her. "Do you not fear me at all?"

She shook her head. "I do not."

"You should."

A line appeared between her brows as she watched him. "Do you want me to fear you?"

Did he? "No, I do not," he said honestly.

The line disappeared, and a faint smile came to her lips. "Then I propose we create an alliance of sorts."

He crossed his arms over his chest. "An alliance? For what purpose?"

"I will go to London," she paused, "willingly, and together we will attend the dreaded Social Season. But if I do not agree to a courtship, then I will return home to Brighton Hall until the following Season."

Nicholas regarded her for a long moment. "I cannot agree to your terms..." He held up his hand when Penelope opened her mouth to protest. "Hear me out first, *woman*." He lowered his hand. "You require a companion, and I feel that it would be mutually beneficial for you to stay on with my mother. I will ask her if she would be willing to spend a few months at Brighton Hall, assuming you choose not to marry."

Penelope's face remained expressionless, but her eyes lit up. "I agree to those terms," she replied calmly.

"Good." The corners of his mouth twitched. "You will learn that I can be reasonable when presented with a good argument." His eyes roamed over her orange dress as he asked, "May I ask where you found that dress?"

She extended the sides of the skirt out. "It was my mother's. She wore it for a costume ball."

"Did she go as a pumpkin?"

Penelope laughed, and an unfamiliar sensation washed over him. "Perhaps," she answered.

Nicholas glanced out the window and noted the sun's position. "It is much too dangerous to depart for London so late in the day. Why don't you change, and we can talk over dinner?"

"I would like that, your grace," she replied with a curtsy.

"I would prefer if you would call me Nicholas."

She smiled brightly at him. "Then you must call me Penelope."

He bowed. "I would be honored, Penelope."

Nicholas walked over to the door and held it open. As Penelope passed through, she offered him a tentative smile before heading towards the stairs.

Not only was his ward beautiful, but she held an inner strength that he had rarely seen in a woman. She did not cower in front of him, nor did she retreat at his first glare. She stood up to him, defending her position. He wasn't sure how he felt about that.

One thing was abundantly clear... this Season was going to be anything but boring.

Dressed in a puce-colored, high-waisted gown with puffy sleeves, Penelope gracefully descended the stairs and headed towards the drawing room. She was proud that she had fought her first battle with her guardian, and although she hadn't technically won, they had struck a truce. True, she would be forced to endure a Season, but she would be allowed to pick her own suitor. That was a win in her book.

Rich, baritone voices could be heard coming out of the drawing room. Her heart fluttered when she heard the duke's voice. That was an odd reaction, considering she was confident that she detested the man. He was condescending and arrogant, but he had shown compassion to her. He could have dismissed her arguments and her, but he allowed her to speak for herself. Perhaps he wasn't all bad.

As she walked into the drawing room, Nicholas and Lord

Northampton rose from their chairs near the fireplace, holding snifters in their hands.

"Gentlemen," she greeted with a smile. "I just spoke to the cook and dinner will be ready shortly."

Nicholas lifted his brow. "You spoke to the cook?" he asked in a way that implied he found her behavior deplorable.

"Is that a problem?"

"Do you not employ a housekeeper?"

She frowned at the question. "I do, but Mrs. Cooley was occupied with another task." The stern disapproval in the duke's eyes caused her pause. "I see that you do not approve of me speaking to my servants."

He took a sip of his drink before acknowledging, "It is below your station to engage with your kitchen staff. You maintain a housekeeper and butler for that purpose."

"How very pompous of you," she replied curtly.

Nicholas' eyes narrowed. "You are an impertinent thing. It would be wise of you to learn to curb your tongue when in a man's presence."

Her mouth gaped. Did he just say that to her? Good heavens! Her guardian was a barbarian. She turned to leave the room when he said, "You are not dismissed."

She slowly turned back around, debating about challenging him to a duel for his haughty behavior. "Dismissed, your grace?" she mocked. "You are treating me like a prisoner in my own home."

Lord Northampton wore a look of amusement on his face as he regarded the duke. "I must agree with Miss Foster, Nicholas. You are acting quite boorish and pretentious."

"Penelope must learn her place," Nicholas remarked.

Heaving a sigh, Lord Northampton turned his gaze back towards her. "Ignore my friend's cantankerous mood." His eyes roamed approvingly over the length of her body. "You are looking beautiful this evening."

"Thank you, my lord," she acknowledged.

He shook his head. "No 'my lord' for you. Please call me Everett. After all, I have no doubt that we will become dear friends."

"She will not call you by your given name," the duke stated. "It is improper."

Everett winked at her as a smile came to his lips.

Feeling a need to prod the duke, she said, "Thank you, Everett."

Before Nicholas could respond, Mr. Watts stepped into the room and announced dinner.

The duke set his snifter down and walked up to her. "Allow me to escort you into the dining room," he said, offering his arm.

Tentatively, she placed her hand onto his sleeve. "Thank you, your grace."

"Nicholas," he reminded her.

Penelope gave him a weak smile as he led her towards the dining room across the hall. Nicholas escorted her to her seat and pulled out the chair.

"Thank you," she murmured as she sat down.

Nicholas pushed in her chair and sat down at the head of the table as Everett sat across from her.

"Nicholas has informed me that you just returned from finishing school," Everett said, breaking the uncomfortable silence that had descended over the group.

Penelope nodded. "It's true. I returned home to Brighton Hall last month."

"And what a grand estate it is," Everett replied, his eyes scanning the rich wood paneling on the walls and the ornate paintings on the ceilings.

"This estate is quite large, and is a fine example of Elizabethan architecture, but, more importantly, it is my home. My haven. This is where my mother taught me how to paint on the east lawn and would read to me in the evenings." Her eyes drifted towards the window. "It's also where my father spent hours teaching me how to ride. In the evenings, I would sit in his office while he balanced his ledgers."

Everett's eyes crinkled in kindness. "It sounds surreal."

"It was... perfect," Penelope murmured, lowering her gaze towards her lap.

How she missed her parents! She would give everything that she had to spend one more day with them... or even one more moment. She was only twelve when they died in a boating accident. A day of leisure on a pleasure boat had turned into a day of tragedy for her.

"I am sorry for your loss," Nicolas stated with warmth in his tone. "I can only imagine the devastation of losing both parents, especially at such a young age."

Penelope brought her gaze up to meet his and was surprised to see the depth of compassion in his eyes. "Thank you."

He held her gaze as he shared, "I have lost too many people that I care about to count."

"I am sorry for your losses," she said.

"Thank you," he responded, clearing his throat, "but death is inevitable. It is the only thing we can plan on with certainty in this life."

"What you say is true," she remarked as she reached for her glass. "But can anyone truly prepare for the void that is left in their hearts when a loved one passes?"

"Not everyone mourns as deeply as you," Nicholas replied. "Besides, death is a reminder that our time on this earth is limited."

Penelope took a moment to ponder what he'd just said. On the surface, his words sounded callous, but she sensed deeper pain behind them. "I agree. Which is why I choose to value my relationships and show gratitude for what I have been blessed with."

A footman placed a plate in front of Nicholas as he replied

mockingly, "Pray tell, what relationships have you cultivated in your young age?"

She saw Everett shoot the duke an annoyed look before she shared, "At the finishing school I attended, I became incredibly close to three other students. They helped me as I grieved the loss of my parents."

"Did these other girls know that you are an heiress and owner of an immensely profitable importing and exporting business?" the duke asked.

"They know I'm an heiress. We kept no secrets from one another," she said, reaching for a fork.

Nicholas cut a piece of his meat. "It would be wise for you not to divulge those kinds of secrets to the women in the ton. They are a gossipy bunch that enjoy the ruination of others and therefore should not be trusted."

Her eyes darted towards Everett. "Then why should I go to such a noxious environment?"

"That is where one goes to find a suitable spouse," the duke responded.

She furrowed her brows. "Do you intend to find a bride amongst those vile women that you speak so callously of?"

He chewed his meat deliberately. "I do not intend to marry."

"Then why do you insist that I must marry?" she countered.

"Because you are a woman," he said, pointing his fork at her.

She opened her mouth to object when Everett asked, "Do you miss the finishing school?"

Turning her gaze towards him, she answered, "At times. I do miss my friends, but we have corresponded with each other on a few occasions." She took a moment to enjoy a sip of water. "I will miss the headmistress and her family. They were gracious enough to allow me to spend the holidays and breaks with them."

"You spent your holidays with the headmistress?" Everett questioned. "Did you have nowhere else to go?"

She shook her head. "No. The duke insisted that I remain at the school and never sent for me during the holidays."

"That is… awful," Everett remarked as he pressed his lips together in a disapproving line.

Penelope put on a brave face. "It was lonely at times, but I had no choice in the matter."

The duke's voice spoke up from the head of the table. "Mr. Fulton informed me that your uncle was a known gambler, and my uncle feared for your safety."

"I doubt that. I was nothing more than a burden to him," she argued.

Nicholas' eyes seemed to bore into hers as he said, "As my ward, you are entitled to always have a place in my home."

"Thank you," she found herself saying.

Penelope found it oddly satisfying hearing those words from him, even though she had no doubt that he said them begrudgingly.

However, it was fun to pretend she belonged somewhere.

4

NICHOLAS ADJUSTED HIS GREEN RIDING JACKET AS HE WALKED down the exterior steps of Brighton Hall. He took a moment to admire the pair of Yorkshire coach horses that would be pulling his posh coach. The trunks had been loaded and footmen were assembled to join them on their trip to London. Everett was speaking to the driver on the coach box but tilted his head in acknowledgement when he met his eye.

A footman approached him, and extended the reins to his horse, Magnus. He accepted the reins as he ran his hand down his horse's neck.

Everett walked over to him. "If all goes well, we will be stopping at a reputable coaching inn for the evening," he announced.

"That's good. I want to…" He stopped speaking when he heard an angelic laugh.

Turning towards the main entry, he saw Penelope and her lady's maid descending the stairs, completely engrossed in chatter. His ward was dressed in a dark blue traveling gown and wearing a straw bonnet, tied loosely below her chin. Blast it! She was exquisite! His life would have been much simpler if Penelope had been a plain looking wallflower. Even without her inheritance, her beauty would ensure she would be highly admired amongst the ton.

Perhaps it would be best if he left Penelope at Brighton Hall for the Season. His eyes traveled over the massive four-level medieval castle. She would be safe here while he could gain his bearings as the Duke of Blackbourne. Then he would send for her the following Season.

Penelope smiled at something that Everett said, and he realized that he couldn't do that to her. He couldn't stifle her, even if she thought it was in her best interest to remain home. He could tell that she was capable of much greater things than hiding away on her estate.

Her smile dimmed as she acknowledged him with a tip of her head. "Morning, your grace."

"Morning, Penelope," he replied, attempting to ignore her lukewarm reception to him. For some reason, it bothered him greatly.

As if she read his thoughts, Penelope approached him, but his feelings soured when she asked, "Would it be permissible if I ride alongside you and Everett?"

"You do not wish to ride inside of the coach with your lady's maid?" he asked, glancing over her shoulder at her lady's maid who was being assisted into the coach by a footman.

Penelope reached out and ran her gloved hand down the length of Magnus' neck. "No. I would prefer to ride."

"It is not appropriate for a woman of your status to ride outside the carriage," he informed her.

Stepping closer, she wore a playful grin on her lips. "No one would know but us."

"You will discover that rules are vital to govern a dignified society. Without rules, our society would plunge into chaos," he stated in a firm tone.

"Although, some rules are outdated and should be reformed,"

she countered. "Besides, I am asking only to ride my horse alongside you. I am not requesting to go to university."

Nicholas saw a groom approach Penelope with her horse already saddled. Her request was a simple one, but he could not allow it. If she continued to get her way, then she would come to expect it. And a spoiled ward was unacceptable. "My answer is *no*. You will ride inside the coach with your lady's maid."

The thin line between her eyebrows appeared. "May I ask why?"

No, you may not, he wanted to shout. Instead, he replied, "It is safer for you to travel inside."

"But I am an accomplished rider and riding in the coach brings back …"

He cut her off. "Enough! I have made my decision."

Penelope stepped back, hurt visible on her delicate features. She handed off her horse to an awaiting footman before stepping into the coach.

Everett came to stand next to him. Once the coach door was closed, he asked, "That was a little harsh, was it not?"

"It is the only way she will learn proper decorum." Nicholas went to mount his horse. "Ruination for a woman amongst the ton could be for the simplest infraction. I will not have that happen to my ward."

Placing his weight in the stirrup, Everett gave him an annoyed look before he mounted his horse. "You are expecting her to act like one of your crew."

"What's wrong with that?" he pressed. "My crew was hailed for its bravery and fought valiantly against the French."

"Your crew did not contain an eighteen-year-old heiress."

He scoffed as he urged his horse forward. "If you think you could do better, then by all means, take Penelope."

"You don't mean that." Everett pointed towards the moving coach. "That girl is counting on you to do right by her."

Nicholas tightened his hold on the reins in his right hand.

"She is not a girl, but a woman. What do I know of being a guardian to a woman?"

"For starters, you can stop shouting at the poor thing," his friend contended. "Be her guardian, not her jailer."

"How else is she supposed to learn proper decorum?"

Everett turned in his saddle to look at him. "You are acting like a ninnyhammer. It is time for you to accept that you are no longer a captain in the Royal Navy. That season of life is over. You are now the Duke of Blackbourne, and you have a ward to take care of. Stop treating Miss Foster so abominably and show her the respect that she deserves."

Nicholas grimaced at the truth of his friend's words. The only reason he returned home was because the Navy Board decommissioned him. They cited his title disqualified him from his work as a captain.

"I had no qualms with issuing orders to my crew," he replied. "They listened and complied, without hesitation. But women, especially Penelope, are a mystery to me. They deal in emotions and feelings, and I can't make any sense of it."

Everett bobbed his head in understanding. "Your mother can ensure Penelope has been taught all the social graces required. Besides, I have no doubt that the finishing school taught her well."

"Then what will my role be?" he asked, keeping his eyes firmly on the coach up ahead.

"Her protector, her friend. Treat her as an equal, not an inferior," his friend advised. "Demonstrate to Miss Foster that you are a gentleman."

"What if Penelope gets out of line?"

Everett grew serious. "You would have no choice but to cane her."

He jerked his head towards his friend. "You heard that?"

"The whole estate heard that," Everett teased. "I must admit she was believable. I truly thought she was partially blind and a bit odd."

Nicholas let out a small chuckle. "I did as well. She could have a career in theatre."

Everett kept his knowing gaze on him. "Miss Foster is a beautiful woman, with or without spectacles."

"I hardly noticed," he mumbled.

"You hardly noticed?" Everett joked.

Having no desire to continue this ridiculous conversation, Nicholas kicked his horse into a run. Penelope was his ward. He wasn't supposed to notice her engaging personality or how her eyes lit up when she smiled.

No. He definitely was not supposed to notice those things.

Penelope's head bumped up against the wall of the coach as it jerked to a stop. So much for getting some rest, she thought. She took a moment to smooth out the wrinkles in her traveling gown.

The door opened, and a footman assisted her out of the coach. She heard loud, boisterous male voices coming from inside the coaching inn, and she found herself searching the courtyard for Nicholas. Despite his stern demeanor, she had no doubt that he would keep her safe and protected.

As if he knew she was searching for him, Nicholas walked out of the coaching inn and headed straight for her, his gaze never wavering.

"We have rented rooms on the third level. You will be sharing a room with your lady's maid for propriety's sake," he informed her.

Penelope turned and saw Claire being assisted out of the coach.

"Allow me to escort you inside," Nicholas said, drawing her attention back to him.

He extended his arm, and she placed her hand on his sleeve. "Thank you," she murmured.

The duke led her into the building. The main hall was filled with men sitting around long tables, holding tankards. Some of the men winked lewdly at her, and she found herself leaning into Nicholas. He must have felt her shudder, because he brought his other hand up and placed it over hers.

"You need not fear. I will keep you safe," he assured her.

Hearing those words caused her to relax, but she remained close to him. Nicholas headed towards a door in the back of the hall and opened it. He stood aside as she passed through and saw a small private dining room.

"I have ordered supper to be brought in," he informed her, closing the door behind him.

"I am famished," she said as she sat down in the chair he offered her.

Nicholas nodded in acknowledgement. "I assumed as much. I also ordered a bath to be brought up to your room after supper."

"Thank you. That is most kind of you," she remarked, surprised by his thoughtfulness.

He pulled out a chair next to her and sat down. "I am glad that we have a moment to speak privately. Everett has brought it to my attention that I have been treating you unfairly." He hesitated, looking entirely unsure of himself. "I would like to apologize."

Penelope tilted her head as she considered her guardian. He appeared genuine. "I thank you for that," she said. "This is new for both of us."

The door opened, and Everett entered. He spied the empty table and frowned. "Where is our supper?"

"The innkeeper said it would be served shortly," Nicholas replied.

Everett went around to the other side of the table and pulled out a chair. "It looks like we are sharing a room, your grace," he stated.

"I daresay sharing a room with you couldn't be worse than sleeping in rat-ridden, lice-infested chambers with hundreds of men," Nicholas replied, smirking.

How was that possible? "But you are a duke," Penelope commented in bewilderment.

Before he could reply, two serving girls brought in trays of bread, cheese, and thinly sliced meat. They placed it on the center of the table and departed.

Everett reached out and plopped a piece of cheese into his mouth. "Before Nicholas was a high and mighty duke, he was a captain in the Royal Navy and commanded his own frigate."

"Do you miss serving in the Royal Navy?" she asked.

A wistful expression came across Nicholas' face. "Every single day."

"How long did you serve?" she pressed.

"Eight years." He ripped off a chunk of bread and extended it towards her. "Eat up."

Penelope accepted the bread and took a bite.

"Nicholas' exploits are legendary," Everett shared. "His tactics were aggressive, and he had an eye for seeing opportunity and taking calculated risks. He was known for his daring rescues and for capturing four French ships."

Her eyes grew wide. "You defeated four French ships?"

"My crew did," Nicholas corrected. "Without the support of a brave crew, willing to follow even the simplest command, a frigate skipper is rendered ineffective."

"You seem young to be a captain," she said boldly.

"I am twenty-eight," he replied, wiping the bread crumbs off his hands. "How old do you suppose captains are?"

46

Penelope opened her mouth to respond when she saw a twinkle in his eye. Nicholas was teasing her in his own stoic way. Two can play at this game, she thought. She reached for a piece of meat while saying, "I always imagined a captain to be old, with white hair, and a pudgy belly."

"A pudgy belly?" he asked with an uplifted brow.

She nodded. "Yes, from all the biscuits they eat."

He studied her with amused eyes. "I'm afraid you don't know the first thing about the Royal Navy."

"It sounds accurate to me," Everett stated in a jovial tone.

Nicholas placed his right forearm on the table as he revealed, "It is true that I am young for a captain, but biscuits are rarely served aboard a frigate."

"That is disappointing," she replied dramatically.

"I purchased a commission when I was twenty, and I became a lieutenant aboard the HMS *Victorious*," Nicholas shared, returning to a more serious tone. "About four years ago, we were involved in a horrific battle. We lost over half of the crew, including the captain and lieutenant commanders above me." He hesitated, before adding, "The French were relentless that day. After bombarding our ship with unyielding cannon blasts, they eventually were able to board us. What ensued after was a fight for our lives."

She leaned forward in her seat, engrossed in his story. "What happened?"

"Yes, what happened?" Everett pressed.

Pursing his lips, Nicholas stared straight ahead, a look of intense contemplation in his eyes. "After our captain was killed, the French expected us to surrender, but I was able to rally the men. We were not just fighting for our lives, but for the lives of every British citizen." His voice grew deeper, more sorrowful. "The crew fought valiantly that day. We ended up defeating the French and capturing their warship. As a reward for my actions on that day, I was promoted to captain and given command over HMS *Victorious*."

She gazed at him in awe. "You are a hero."

"No," came his quick reply. "I did what I was trained to do. Nothing more."

Penelope was baffled. Why would the duke be so quick to dismiss her comment that he was a hero? His actions clearly indicated he was. Unexpectedly, a yawn sneaked past her lips, and she brought her hand up to cover her mouth. "Excuse me. I must be more tired than I realize."

"Did you not sleep in the coach?" Nicholas asked.

She shook her head. "No. To be honest, the coach brings back horrible memories. Closing my eyes only worsens the situation."

"What is it about being inside of a coach that brings back these bad memories?" Everett inquired in concern.

"The day after my parent's funeral, which was also my thirteenth birthday, I was placed into a coach with an elderly woman that I had never met before, and we traveled north to the finishing school. Mrs. Hansen allowed me to cry for one hour after we left, but after that, she chastised me if I grew emotional," she explained softly. "Within a short period of time, I lost my parents, my home, and my entire way of life. It was just stripped away, and for a brief time, I wondered if I had just imagined it."

"Is that why you wanted to ride outside of the coach?" Nicholas questioned, his tone holding an edge to it.

"It was," she murmured, keeping her gaze lowered.

Nicholas placed his elbows onto his legs and leaned closer. "Why did you not say anything before?"

"I tried, but you ordered me into the coach," she responded, lifting her gaze to meet his.

He wasn't smiling at her, but he wasn't frowning either.

Instead, he appeared to be studying her. "If we want this to work, we need honesty between us."

Penelope nodded, and the corners of his mouth lifted. "I would like that, your gra... Nicholas."

"Good." Nicholas took his hand and wiped his chin thoughtfully. "You still need to follow the rules of decorum, but perhaps we can come to an agreement."

"Another alliance?" she teased with a smile.

"I will allow you to ride with us until we near London," he paused, holding up his hand. "Then, you must complete the journey in the coach for propriety's sake."

Penelope sat straight in her seat. "I can agree to those terms wholeheartedly."

"Excellent," he replied, maintaining her gaze. "Should we finish eating our supper?"

Her smile grew. "I think that is a grand idea."

For the briefest of moments, she thought Nicholas would return her smile, but he cleared his throat and tore his gaze away from hers.

Nicholas was an anomaly. His exterior was hardened, but he continually surprised her with acts of kindness. What would it take to see him smile?

☙ 5 ❧

"You milked a cow?" Lord Northampton asked bluntly.

"I did," Penelope answered as she rode between the two lords. "It is quite simple," she hesitated, "once you get the hang of it." She snuck a glance at Nicholas and his expression revealed nothing. Not even the disapproval she suspected. Good heavens, she thought. Did the man ever show emotion?

They had been traveling for hours, trailing behind the coach, and Nicholas had yet to say a word, other than the occasional grunt. Why did he refuse to engage in conversation with them? Everett had regaled her with stories about his time at Eton, and she found herself thoroughly entertained. How did these two lords become friends? One was aloof and boorish, whereas the other was engaging and charming.

"The headmistress allowed you to milk the cow?" Everett asked, drawing her attention back.

She shook her head. "Heavens, no."

"Then how did you find yourself on a stool in front of a cow's udder?" he joked.

Tightening her hold on the reins, she replied, "I was granted permission to teach Sarah, a young kitchen servant, how to read, but her studying was not to interfere with her daily chores. It was only logical that I wake up early to help assist her with her morning chores, so we had more time to study before breaking our fast."

"Did you hear that Nicholas?" Everett asked, turning his amused gaze towards his friend. "Your ward taught a servant how to read and woke up early to assist with the morning chores."

Nicholas clenched his jaw. "I have ears."

Ignoring the duke's reaction, Penelope continued her story with pride. "By the time I left for home, Sarah could read and write fluently, and I often found her reading in the library. I have no doubt that she could work her way up to becoming a teacher at the finishing school one day."

"You did a good service for that servant," Everett remarked. "It is rare for people to rise above their stations."

Uncomfortable with praise, Penelope attempted to downplay the significance. "Sarah was the one who took the initiative by asking me to tutor her. It showed true bravery on her part, if you ask me."

Nicholas turned his stern glare towards her, and she anticipated a rebuke. However, to her astonishment, he said, "To show compassion to someone less fortunate is expected, but giving of your time and talents to serve them demonstrates charity. And that is a fine quality to possess."

Penelope stared at him for a moment before acknowledging, "Thank you."

Nicholas nodded before turning his head back towards the road and watched as the coach crested a small hill ahead of them.

Hoping to engage him in conversation, she asked, "What was your childhood like?"

"Lonely," came his gruff reply.

"Surely, it could not have been that bad," she pressed.

His jaw clenched and a muscle below his ear started pulsating. "I never granted you permission to ask such personal questions."

Everett sighed. "It is best if you don't try to antagonize him, Penelope. Nicholas is being rather testy today."

Just today? She shook off the unkind thought as she turned back towards Lord Northampton. "Did you have a pleasant childhood?"

He grinned. "I did. I grew up with two younger brothers and a sister. We ran my parents ragged with our shenanigans."

"Is that so?" she asked.

With mirth in his eyes, Everett shared, "We spent our summers outside, playing in the trees, and swimming in a pond near our estate. My brothers and I even crafted a boat, and we used it to go fishing."

"That is impressive," she expressed.

Everett chuckled. "It was for the first few moments. However, once we reached the middle of the pond, the boat started taking in water. We had to abandon our ship and swim back to shore with our fishing lines."

Penelope's chestnut mare nickered and tossed its head, causing her to giggle. "It appears that Mildred thought your story was amusing as well."

"You named your horse Mildred?" Nicholas huffed as Everett let out a loud laugh. "That is not a fitting name for a horse."

Not taking offense, she replied, "My father allowed me to name the mare when it was born. I thought it looked like a Mildred when I was ten."

She eyed Nicholas' black stallion. "Pray tell, what is the name of your horse?"

"Magnus," he responded, curtly.

Determined to break through his tough exterior, she asked, "Have you had Magnus for long?"

Nicholas took his hand and affectionately petted the horse. "I have. Magnus goes wherever I go."

Confused, she pressed, "But weren't you a captain of a ship?"

He nodded. "It was not uncommon for war ships to travel with horses."

Touched by the love he had for his horse, she expressed, "That is endearing that you and your horse share such a unique bond."

Nicholas tensed. "There is nothing endearing about it. If I must go ashore, I require a competent horse."

Ah, he's practical, she thought. "And no other horse would be up for that task?" she asked innocently.

A hint of vulnerability came to his eyes before he blinked it away. "If you must know, Magnus was my brother's horse."

"You have a brother?"

"Had," he corrected harshly. "He died."

She offered him a sad smile. "I am sorry for your loss."

Nicholas stroked the horse again. "By keeping Magnus near, it is like I have a connection to my brother."

"I understand," she replied. "Mildred was a gift from my father and a daily reminder of how much he loved me."

He looked over at her with sadness on his features and something passed between them. For a brief moment, they acknowledged each other's pain and sorrow, not in words, but in silence.

Nicholas opened his mouth, but then closed it quickly. He turned his direction back towards the road, and declared, "We are nearing London. It is time for you to finish the remainder of our trip in the coach."

Her eyes scanned the horizon, and she saw no signs of the great city up ahead. "Just a few more moments?" she asked, fearful of his rejection.

He nodded. "As you wish."

Nicholas reined in his horse in front of Hereford Hall, his townhouse on Grosvenor Street. It was a stately three-level, red brick structure, with a high four-column portico at the main entry, and large windows.

Hereford Hall now belonged to him. His eyes scanned around the pristine gardens and the well-polished exterior. Why did he find no joy in his possessions? He already knew the answer. He had robbed his brother, Alfred, of his rightful place as duke. This all should have belonged to him.

Miss Foster exited the carriage and waited politely for him as he dismounted his horse. As he extended his reins to the groomsman, Nicholas saw her eyes glancing nervously towards the main door before she began to wring her hands together.

He approached her and asked, "What is wrong?"

Her hands stilled, and any hint of nervousness vanished. "Why do you suppose something is wrong?"

Giving her a knowing look, he remained silent, hoping she would confide her feelings.

Taking a step closer to him, Penelope lowered her voice as she admitted, "If you must know, I'm nervous."

One side of his lips curled up. "You, nervous?"

She visibly relaxed at his teasing tone. "It is much easier to be strong when someone is familiar with their surroundings. Here…" she held up her hand towards Hereford Hall, "I don't belong."

Nicholas knew exactly what she spoke of. "I know what you mean. This townhouse, the title, and prestige was supposed to belong to others, not me. Yet, here I am. And here you are."

"What if your mother doesn't like me?" she asked, nibbling her bottom lip. "I know I can be a bit odd."

"Odd?" He shook his head. "You are uniquely perfect, Penelope. Let no one make you feel inferior."

Her wide, expressive eyes were guarded. "Are you sure I can't return home and wait till next Season?"

"That would be easier," he agreed, "but the easiest path is generally the wrong path." He hesitated, before adding, "You need not fret. I will be by your side."

"Thank you," she acknowledged, her words full of gratitude. "It is nice not to make this journey alone."

His eyes met hers. "I agree." He extended his arm towards her. "Shall we?"

Everett's cheery voice came from behind him. "Oh good. I was waiting for you and Penelope to stop conversing."

He turned his head towards his friend. "Why are you still here? Kindly leave and go to your own townhouse."

"I want to enjoy the pleasure of your company for a little bit longer," his friend stated with a smile on his face.

Nicholas huffed. "I highly doubt that. I suspect it has something to do with my French chef, Monsieur Bisset."

"Perhaps," Everett replied as he stopped at the door to allow Penelope to enter first.

Taking a step into the entrance hall of Hereford Hall, Nicholas was amazed at the splendor of it all. Painted mauve columns framed the doors, alcoves displayed works of art and other treasures, the ceiling held intricate designs and the floor had been crafted from the finest stone. Also visible from the main entrance hall was a dominating staircase that swept up in a sumptuous curve to the floor above.

"Nicholas," his mother's voice called out as she glided down the stairs. "You are finally home."

Penelope went to remove her hand from his arm, but he reached out and placed his hand firmly over hers. Whether she needed his support, or he needed hers, he knew not. But having Penelope close by felt reassuring.

His mother, the Duchess of Blackbourne, stopped in front of him with a wide smile on her face. "You are looking well, my boy."

Nicholas acknowledged her comment with a tilt of his head. "As are you, Mother." He noted that time had been kind to her. Despite her hair turning silver, she still had the same slim face with hardly any wrinkles.

Everett stepped forward and bowed while murmuring, "Your grace."

"Everett, thank you for bringing my Nicholas home," his mother said, before turning her expectant gaze to Penelope. "Who might this be?"

"Miss Penelope Foster, allow me to introduce you to my mother, Mildred Dallison, the Duchess of Blackbourne," Nicholas stated, enjoying the moment when Penelope discovered his mother and her horse shared the same name. "Miss Foster is my ward."

His mother's eyes darted to his. "Your ward?"

"I take it that Father didn't mention Miss Foster to you, either?" Nicholas asked dryly.

"Your father and I did not speak very often, especially towards the end."

Nicholas felt like a cad as soon as he saw his mother's crestfallen expression. He cleared his throat. "I was hoping you would introduce Miss Foster into society."

That was the right thing to say, because a smile came to his mother's face. "I would be honored," she replied, her eyes roaming over his ward. "You are exquisite, my dear."

Miss Foster returned her smile. "Thank you, your grace..." Her voice trailed off as she removed her hand from his and dropped into a curtsy. "My apologies. I assure you that I have been taught social etiquette. I'm afraid I am more nervous than I previously thought."

His mother, always the gracious hostess, walked up to Miss

Foster and placed a hand on her right shoulder. "There will be no formalities with us," she leaned in, "at least not in private. I insist that you call me Mildred. For I have no doubt that we will become fast friends."

Leaning closer to Penelope, Everett teased, "Mildred is a fantastic name for a friend, is it not?"

Ignoring him, Miss Foster flashed the duchess a relieved smile. "I would very much like that. I don't have too many friends."

"No?" his mother asked in surprise. "And why is that?"

Nicholas spoke up before Penelope could answer. "Miss Foster was sent to Miss Bell's Finishing School for Young Ladies after the death of her parents, Sir Charles and Lady Edith Foster."

His mother's eyes widened with recognition. "You are the daughter of Sir Charles Foster?" she asked in a slow voice before her eyes lit up in excitement. "Oh dear, we are going to have such fun this Season. Such fun, indeed!" Her hands waved in front of her. "Gentlemen callers will be coming in and out of our drawing room. We might even need to draw straws for them to call on you."

"Absolutely not," Nicholas roared, causing Penelope to jump. "She is not to receive any gentleman callers until they have spoken to me first."

"But, Nicholas…" his mother started.

He cut her off. "This is not up for debate."

"I understand," Mildred replied.

Nicholas stepped closer to his ward. "You should know that Penelope and I have reached an agreement. I have given her leave to pick her own suitor, assuming he is worthy of her."

His mother brought a hand up to cover her smile as she glanced over at Everett with amusement on her features. "I see," she said. "So, I take it that you will be actively involved in your ward's decision."

"Of course. She is my charge," he stated.

The duchess' smile grew, and she dropped her hand. "This Season is definitely going to be interesting," she remarked. "Now, Penelope. Follow me. I will show you to your bedchamber, and we are going to have a nice chat before supper." She directed her attention to Everett. "Please say you will be staying for supper."

Everett bowed. "I wouldn't miss it, your grace."

"Excellent," the duchess replied.

❧ 6 ❧

PENELOPE KEPT HER STEPS LIGHT AS SHE HURRIED ALONG THE expansive hall and headed straight towards the servant's entrance that led down to the kitchen. Other than an occasional knowing smile, none of the servants gave her much heed as she hurried down the stairs and out the back door.

At last, she was free. She felt like spinning in a circle at the joy of being out of the estate. But it was much too soon to rejoice. Maintaining her quick stride, she didn't stop until she arrived at the stable. The duchess would eventually notice that she wasn't resting in her bedchamber. She had claimed fatigue during a tutorial on the required seating arrangements during a social gathering and asked to be allowed to rest before learning the rules of social calls.

Penelope stepped through the stable doors and continued walking down the hall until she found her horse's stall. She unlatched the door and stepped inside, closing it behind her.

"Mildred," she said, removing an apple from the pocket of her gown. "How I have missed you!"

After Mildred finished eating the apple, she nuzzled up against her, which warmed Penelope's heart. How she loved this horse! Luckily, the duchess hadn't discovered that she shared the same name as her horse.

Mildred whinnied, drawing her attention back. What if she took Mildred for a ride? Neither Nicholas nor the duchess had specifically forbidden her to ride her horse. They had only informed her that she was never allowed to leave the estate without an escort. The north side of Hereford Halls had rolling green hills and was wide enough for her to gallop to her heart's content. She would just ride out, stay on the duke's land, and no one would ever know.

With her decision made, she glanced into the passageway and saw grooms mucking out empty stalls. It wouldn't be fair of her to ask them to stop working to saddle Mildred, especially since she could competently tack up her own horse.

Penelope attached the lead rope to the bridle, unlatched the stall door and opened it wide enough to lead Mildred out into the center of the stable. "Allow me to assist you, Miss," a groom said, placing his shovel against the wall.

"Not necessary, but thank you," Penelope replied as she secured the lead to a hook on the wall. Picking up a brush off a stool, she began brushing Mildred down.

The groomsman wiped his hands on his trousers as he approached her, saying, "It's no trouble at all, miss. I am quick at tacking up horses."

"You are kind, but I would like to do this myself," she asserted as she continued to brush in fluid strokes.

He stuffed his hands in his pockets, a frown puckered on his lips. "I don't think his grace would approve."

Placing the brush back on the stool, she replied, "If you insist on helping, would you mind bringing over my side saddle?"

The groomsman rushed to do her bidding just as the duke's angry voice echoed throughout the stable. "What do you think you are doing, Miss Foster?"

"I think it's fairly obvious," she responded, not deterred by his anger. She placed a small blanket on her horse before the groom placed the side saddle on top. "How did you even know I was here?"

"I saw you running past my study window." Nicholas pointed at her gown. "You're not even dressed in proper riding attire."

Frowning, she acknowledged that he did have a point. She was wearing a muslin gown since she hadn't planned to ride Mildred. Her riding habit was made from much sturdier material, but she hadn't taken time to go change. "This gown will be sufficient to ride on your lands. It's cut long enough."

Nicholas stormed towards her, his glare intensifying with each step. "Ladies do not saddle their own horses. I demand that you allow the groom to finish tacking your horse."

Her horse pawed at the straw-coated ground as if she sensed her irritation. "I will not," Penelope stated firmly. "It has been four days since we arrived at Hereford Hall, and I have yet to ride Mildred."

"That is because you have been busy with lessons from my mother," he pointed out.

"I'm going mad, Nicholas. Truly, utterly mad," she informed him, reaching under the horse's belly and retrieving the strap. "I can't take any more lessons."

"Surely, it can't be that bad."

Penelope huffed as she reached for the bridle hanging on a hook. "May I ask how you would know? You are not a lady. Finishing school was a breeze compared to your mother's tutoring. I am starting to dream about social etiquette." Once the bridle was secure on Mildred, she stepped back. "I need some time alone."

"Out of the question," he asserted.

Stepping closer to him, she lowered her voice to keep what she was about to say private. "I need a break from your mother."

"Has my mother been unkind to you?" he asked with concern.

"Oh, heavens no," she rushed out. "Your mother is kind and gracious and..." Her voice trailed off as she placed a hand on Mildred.

"And?" he prodded.

"The duchess reminds me so much of my mother," she replied, blinking back her tears.

His face was unreadable, but his eyes had softened with warmth. "If you will wait for a few hours, I will accompany you," he said gently.

She shook her head in frustration. "Ever since we arrived, you have been hiding out in your study."

"I've been busy."

Penelope arched an eyebrow at him. "For four days?" She turned her attention back to the saddle, tightening the girth and strap again before securing it down. "I highly suspect you are avoiding your mother... and me."

"For what purpose?"

"I don't know. You tell me," she challenged.

Nicholas glanced at her curiously. "How did you learn to saddle a horse?"

"My father taught me," she shared. "He said if I wanted to establish a true bond with Mildred, that I needed to not only ride her but groom her as well."

"It must have been hard for you to leave Mildred behind when you left for finishing school."

She placed her hand on her horse's neck. "It was awful, but I had no choice."

"Be that as it may, it's not appropriate for a woman of your station to saddle a horse," Nicholas said. "You need to think of your reputation now."

Penelope rolled her eyes. "If being a duke does not work out, then you might want to consider being a governess. You have an incredible aptitude for spoiling all the fun."

He crossed his arms over his wide chest. "Now you are just

being temperamental. Perhaps a cup of tea might calm your nerves and help you see reason."

Her mouth opened wide at his idiotic statement. "I can't believe you just said that to me. You know nothing about women, do you?"

Wincing, Nicholas dropped his arms to his side. "That's what I have been trying to tell you all along. But I am trying, Penelope."

"I know. I'm trying too." Her eyes drifted towards the open stable doors. "Do you ever have the desire to get on your horse and ride far, far away?"

"Away from all your burdens and pains?"

She nodded.

"I do all the time."

Penelope smiled mischievously. "Then let's do it now. Your work and responsibility will be there when you get home."

She could see the indecision in his eyes before they grew determined. "We will have to hurry if we want to arrive home before supper," he said, stepping over to Magnus' stall.

"Allow me to help you saddle Magnus…"

Nicholas spoke over her, loudly. "Absolutely not."

Penelope leaned closer to Mildred and whispered, "The duke can be quite temperamental. Perhaps he needs a cup of tea to calm his nerves."

"I can hear you, Miss Foster," the duke growled, and she laughed.

Racing their horses in the fields well beyond Hereford Hall, Nicholas felt energized, alive. It had been so long since he had just stepped away from his burdens, even for a moment.

He glanced over and saw Penelope sitting elegantly on her saddle, smiling. His ward had the most brilliant smile. One that would light up even the darkest night. Somehow, she found reasons to smile even though her past had been filled with heartache and sorrow. How was that possible?

Penelope reined in her horse and pointed towards a small stream. "I think we should give our horses a rest."

"I think that's wise." He urged his horse towards the stream and dismounted. After securing his horse, he turned to assist Penelope as she dismounted.

She placed her hands on his shoulders and allowed him to ease her down to the ground. "Thank you," she murmured sweetly.

He stepped back and reached for her horse's reins. "We are in one of the far corners of Hyde Park," he informed her.

A wistful smile came to Penelope's lips. "My mother told me stories of how my father would take her on long carriage rides through Hyde Park when they were courting." She lowered her tone, as if she was sharing a secret. "My father was even so bold as to sneak kisses before they were married."

Nicholas wanted to laugh at Penelope's exuberance, but he kept his expression neutral. His ward was an innocent. One that needed to be protected from the trappings of Society. That was his job. His duty.

Realizing she was still waiting for his response, he replied, "It is not uncommon for men to seek certain liberties from beautiful young women, such as yourself. You must always use caution, especially from fortune hunters. Some wouldn't think twice about abducting girls to achieve their nefarious purposes."

Penelope's eyes drifted towards a field of red poppy flowers blowing in the wind. "Did you know your mother planned a ball in my honor?"

"I did." At her curious glance, he admitted, "I agreed to pay for it."

"Don't I have the funds to pay for my own ball?"

He let out an amused huff at her naive question. "You have adequate funds, but you are my ward. It is my privilege to host a ball for you."

Penelope's tone started off as unsure, hesitant. "Do you suppose it would be possible to be more involved with my finances? After all, I know nothing about my father's... er... my company."

"I will look into it," he began, "but it is unseemly for a woman to be involved in financial matters, other than pin money and household expenses."

She placed her right hand on her hip. "May I ask why?"

"Women should be more interested in womanly pursuits and rearing children..." His voice trailed off as his ward stormed away. He secured the horses and easily caught up to her. "What do you think you are doing, Miss Foster?"

She defiantly met his gaze. "Do you truly believe the rhetoric coming out of your mouth?"

"We follow society's rules..."

Taking a step closer to him, she asked, "What if I choose not to marry? Am I to live ignorantly about the financial state of my investments?"

He gave her a look of disbelief. "You do not have to fear about becoming a spinster. I guarantee that you will have a long list of suitors vying for your attention."

"Because I am an heiress?" she questioned.

Nicholas nodded. "There is that, but you are also a beautiful young woman."

Penelope crossed her arms over her chest, briefly drawing his attention towards her comely figure. He met her gaze as she pressed, "If I wasn't an heiress, or if I didn't have any type of dowry to speak of, do you still think I would have a long list of suitors?"

"I have no doubt," he asserted.

"But I am more desirable because of my fortune."

Confounded woman. Why was she being so difficult? "What do you expect me to say? To tell you that your fortune means nothing to the gentlemen of the ton? Is that what you want? For me to lie to you?"

"No. But I want to be accepted for who I am, not because of my fortune," she replied, dropping her arms to her sides.

Nicholas gave her a look of pity, mingled with his growing annoyance at the direction of this conversation. "We agreed to be honest with each other, and I would be remiss if I did not give you this piece of advice." She lifted her brow in anticipation of his words. "Men of the ton do not marry for love. They marry to secure their own futures."

Sadness crept into her eyes, but it didn't appear to be a result from his words. It seemed as if she felt sorrow for him. "Is that what you aspire to for your marriage? A marriage of convenience?"

He should have anticipated that question. "I already told you that I do not intend to marry. Ever."

"Why?" she asked in confusion.

"It is a long, complicated story," he responded dismissively.

The line between her brow appeared. "But you are a duke. Don't you require an heir?"

Nicholas shifted his gaze, attempting to avoid her scrutiny. He had made his decision. He didn't need to explain his reasons to anyone... especially his ward.

"The line will pass to my second cousin, Mr. Robert Downsend," he said curtly.

Reaching out, she placed her hand on the sleeve of his blue riding jacket. "Why are you choosing to be lonely, Nicholas?" she asked with sympathy in her tone.

The way his name rolled off her tongue caused him to bring his gaze to her lips. How was it possible that Penelope's piercing gaze managed to look into his soul, rendering him unable to resist her questions? Blast it! He would tell her the truth… well, the partial truth.

Looking down at her hand, he shared, "My father was an arrogant, cruel and abusive man. When I was younger, my mother would attempt to protect Alfred and me from my father's heavy hand, but it only seemed to fuel his anger. He found pleasure in striking us and my mother."

"That's awful," she murmured.

"Fortunately, he spent most of his time at his mistress's townhouse. I was told he even died in her bed." Nicholas opened his mouth to apologize for the brashness of his words, but Penelope interrupted him.

"Is that why you don't want to marry? So you won't repeat the sins of your father?"

Surprised by the directness of her question, he found himself nodding.

She eyed him with concern. "You are not like your father."

"How would you know?" he huffed.

Her face softened as a smile came to her lips. "I have given you ample reason to punish me, but you have never once laid a hand on me."

"That's true. I am not heavy-handed. However, you are wrong about me," he stated. "I am selfish and…" He stopped speaking, knowing he couldn't admit that. He couldn't tell her that he was responsible for his brother's death.

Penelope stepped closer, and he could smell the delightful aroma of rosewater on her. "Behind your gruff exterior, I have seen kindness and compassion. You are not who you claim to be."

Wanting to change the tone of this suddenly serious conversation, he changed tactics. He decided to tease her, and a grin came to his lips. "Careful, it almost sounds like you are complimenting me."

Penelope's gaze lingered on his lips before she brought her eyes up to meet his. "You're smiling."

The smile vanished. "I was not."

"You were," she pointed out.

Nicholas turned his gaze back towards the direction of his estate. "I suppose for the first time in a long time, I have something to smile about," he said honestly.

Penelope started walking back towards their horses. "We should head back so I can practice my embroidery before supper." She smirked over her shoulder. "Your mother said my needlework is 'passable'."

"That's high praise from my mother," he joked.

As he assisted his ward onto her horse, he found himself grateful for her words of support. Everett was right. He was her guardian, but that didn't mean they couldn't be friends.

❦ 7 ❧

Nicholas was sitting at the table in the dining room, enjoying the silence as he read his morning paper. He read each article referencing the war with Napoleon, hoping to find any articles that mentioned his ship, HMS *Victorious*.

The door to the dining room opened and closed in quick precision, but he gave it no heed, assuming it was a servant entering the room. As he continued to read the paper, he heard the door open again, but this time he didn't hear it close.

He lowered the paper and saw Penelope standing at the partially opened door, staring out into the hall. A frown puckered her lips as she kept her hand on the handle. She was dressed in the most alluring pale pink gown with a square neckline, and her hair was piled high on her head with curls framing her face. Her brown curls rested on her shoulder, drawing his attention towards her elegant neck.

With a decisive bob of her head, she closed the door and turned towards him with a triumphant smile on her face.

"Do you want to explain what that was all about?" he asked, looking amused.

Shrugging one shoulder, she replied, "Nothing to concern a duke about."

"I see," he said, folding the paper and placing it onto the table.

Her eyes scanned the buffet table filled with food. "Do you mind if I break my fast with you?"

Nicholas brought up his right hand and snapped his fingers, directing a footman to bring Penelope a plate. "Of course, but I was under the impression that you were eating with my mother in her bedchamber this morning," he stated, rising and pulling out her chair for her.

Penelope kept her eyes on the plate that was being prepared for her. "We were, but I snuck out when your mother wasn't paying attention." When the plate was placed in front of her, her eyes grew wide, and she reached out to grab a pastry. "Are these Bath buns?" she asked as she took a big bite and chewed with pleasure.

"They are." He turned his head to see a plate filled with the pastries at the buffet table. "Would you like another one?"

She nodded and brought her hand up to cover her mouth as she said, "Yes, please."

He attempted to stifle his laugh, but he failed, miserably. "Are we not feeding you enough?"

Penelope finished eating her pastry and reached for her napkin. After wiping her mouth, she lowered it back to her lap. "Your mother," she glanced over her shoulder at the door, "orders me a piece of buttered toast, a boiled egg, and a cup of tea every morning. It is hardly enough food for a bird to live on."

"Did you think of ordering additional food to be sent up to you?" he asked, providing a relatively easy solution to her problem.

A footman approached the table and placed two buns on her plate.

"It is not that simple," she expressed. "The duchess

explained that it is important for young ladies to curb their appetites to avoid an increasingly curvaceous figure."

His eyes discreetly eyed her willowy frame as she bit into the pastry. One would never describe Penelope as being plump.

"Have you told my mother how you feel?"

"No," she replied. "Your mother has been so kind and gracious to tutor me these past few days. I wouldn't dare complain."

Nicholas took his fork and stabbed the remaining bun on her plate.

"What are you doing?" she asked as he yanked back his fork and placed the pastry onto his plate.

He removed his fork and set it down while explaining, "My mother isn't the only one that is qualified to give you lessons."

"What game are you playing?" she asked, eyeing him suspiciously.

Picking up the pastry, he remarked, "If you allow my mother to dictate your actions, I can only imagine how the ton will see your weaknesses and exploit them."

"It's quite different," she contended. "First, I have no desire to insult the duchess, nor do I want to diminish the validity of her lessons."

He brought the bun up to his nose. "You need to stand up for yourself, regardless of the circumstances. Today, it is a delicious pastry, but tomorrow, it could be lewd, untruthful gossip being spread throughout society about you."

"You are prone to exaggeration, I see," she joked.

"Not at all," he asserted. "The ton is full of vipers, members that wish to tear another down, just to build themselves up."

Penelope placed her forearm on the table and leaned closer, her eyes sparking with merriment. "If that is the case, then what is our battle plan?"

"Our battle plan?" He chuckled. "No, my dear, I am not

foolish enough for the trappings of society. I already informed you that I do not seek a wife."

With a coy smile, she said, "You are my guardian, and were the wisest, most handsome captain in all of the Royal Navy. Surely, you can help me navigate Society?" She fluttered her lashes.

Nicholas took a bite of her bun, ignoring her gasp. "Flattery has its limitations and doesn't work on me. You need to learn as much as you can about your opponent and use that to your advantage. Their likes, their dislikes..." His voice trailed off as he snapped his fingers at his footman. "More Bath buns for Miss Foster."

A footman rushed to do his bidding and brought another plate filled with buns. He waved his hand over the pastries. "Would you care for a bun, Penelope?" he asked politely.

"I would," she replied as she brought her hand up to select a pastry.

Nicholas grabbed the plate and moved it out of the way.

She frowned at him.

"Society is waiting for you to make a mistake," he explained. "They will revel in your failures."

Penelope lowered her gaze towards the plate of buns and sighed. "I'm hungry," she murmured softly.

His heart lurched at her simple words, and he pushed the plate of pastries towards her. "I do apologize. I was just taking the opportunity to tease you."

Bringing her eyes up, they were full of humor. "You follow your heart more than you realize."

"You tricked me?"

She smirked as she picked up a pastry. "We both can pretend to be someone we are not."

"Why do you think I am playing a role?" he asked, watching in fascination as she took a bite and licked her bottom lip.

Turning her full attention to him, she revealed, "I can tell that you must have been a remarkable captain, and I have no doubt that your crew trusted you completely."

Surprised by her compliment, he stared at her for a moment. "Why do you say that?"

"A hunch," she replied vaguely.

He lifted his brow. "A hunch?"

"I can't reveal all my secrets, your grace," she teased with a smile.

Nicholas suddenly had a desire to learn all about his ward, and her supposed secrets. "Would you like to go on a walk after breakfast in the gardens?"

Her eyes softened as she opened her mouth to respond. However, before she answered, his mother opened the door and walked into the dining room. She let out a relieved sigh when she saw Penelope.

"Oh good. There you are," she rushed out. "I was worried you snuck off for another ride." She glanced between the two of them. "Why are you in the dining room? Didn't you eat breakfast in my room?"

Penelope turned her head towards the duchess, and he could see her trying to formulate an excuse for being there. "I... um..."

Nicholas spoke over her, taking pity on her. "I was on my way down for breakfast, and I saw Penelope in the hall. I asked her to join me while I break my fast."

With a smile, his mother acknowledged, "That was most kind of you, Nicholas. I know how much you enjoy eating breakfast alone."

"Not anymore," he declared. "I have decided that we must eat breakfast every morning... as a family."

He was rewarded to see Penelope offer him a private smile. A smile that he had no doubt would permeate his thoughts.

"That is wonderful news," the duchess gushed before turning her attention back towards his ward. "We will be departing shortly for town."

LAURA BEERS

"For what purpose?" Nicholas asked, reaching for his tea.

"The gown designed specifically for Penelope to wear to her ball needs final alterations," his mother explained. "The modiste requested the fitting to be done at the shop."

He waved his hand dismissively. "That's nonsense. Pay the additional fee and insist the modiste come to our home."

Turning in her seat to face him, Penelope protested, "I would like to go to town. I haven't been to London in years, and your mother promised that we could get lemon ice."

Nicholas sat back in his seat and contemplated her request. He could send along footmen to protect her, but that wouldn't necessarily ensure her safety. She was protected at Hereford Hall, but he couldn't very well keep her prisoner here.

He pushed back his chair and rose. "All right. I shall escort you to the dress shop."

"You?" his mother questioned. "You wish to go to the modiste?"

"Yes," he replied, tugging down on his waistcoat.

Penelope rose and smiled at him again. "What fun we shall have!" she exclaimed eagerly. "I will go retrieve my shawl."

As his ward left the room, his mother lifted a brow knowingly at him, but was wise enough not to say anything.

He cleared his throat. "Allow me to request the carriage to be brought out front."

"Thank you, son," the duchess replied in an amused tone.

Nicholas tipped his head in acknowledgment as he walked out of the room. Why had he just agreed to go to a dress shop? He had piles of correspondences that he needed to catch up on. He doubted he could finish all the work associated with being a duke in one lifetime. So why was he leaving everything behind to escort his ward into town?

Tarnation! He knew why. He wanted to see her smile again.

Penelope couldn't seem to control her excitement as she exited the modiste's shop on Fleet Street, causing the bell to jingle above the door. The trip had taken longer than anticipated, but she had enjoyed scouring through the samples of ribbons and fine materials.

When Nicholas saw her, he pushed off the shop's wall and approached her. "Please say that you're finally done with your shopping."

"I did warn you that a trip to the modiste could take hours," the duchess reminded him.

"You did," he replied, extending his arms towards them. "I believe I earned some lemon ice for my good behavior."

Penelope accepted his arm, savoring the nearness of him. "I can hardly believe how beautiful the ball gown is that your mother commissioned for me."

"It suits you nicely, my dear," the duchess complimented.

As Nicholas escorted her down the busy pavement, she couldn't help but admire the storefronts. There were hats of all shapes and sizes, ribbons in a wide array of colors, and jewels that sparkled in the light. How she longed to stop and browse each store.

"Is there a specific store you'd like to visit?" Nicholas asked, drawing her attention back towards him.

"No, thank you."

"It would be no bother."

Her eyes drifted back towards a millinery shop. "I apologize. London brings back such fond memories for me. My mother used to take me shopping, and we would spend hours walking around the shops."

"Is that so?" he asked, his expression remaining passive. "Did you have a favorite store?"

She bobbed her head. "Yes. Wrightman's Sweets Shop."

"I should have known it was a candy shop," he teased.

Penelope blinked back the tears at the memory of strolling down the pavement with her mother, licorice in their hands as footmen trailed behind holding their packages.

Nicholas eyed her for a moment before turning towards the bustling street. He waved down a hackney. "Come. We will need to take a hackney if we wish to arrive at Wrightman's before it closes."

She stilled on the pavement when she realized he was in earnest. "That is not necessary, Nic…"

"It is," he insisted as he went to assist her into the hackney.

Smoothing out her dress, she said, "I don't even know if the store is still open."

The duchess sat down next to her. "It is, and it's not far."

Before long they pulled up to the familiar red-painted sign that read 'Wrightman's Sweets Shop'." The storefront may have received a fresh coat of paint, but it was just as she remembered.

Penelope walked into the store and took a deep breath. The smell of the sweets store was strong and overwhelmingly pleasant. She admired the glass containers filled with caramels, toffee, taffy, spun sugar and butterscotches.

A young, lanky man wearing a white apron approached them and asked, "May I help you?"

Nicholas held up an expectant brow at her. "What would you like?"

Her eyes roamed the contents until they landed on the licorice sticks. "I would like a piece of licorice, please."

The young employee bobbed his head in approval. "Excellent choice, Miss. The licorice was made fresh this morning." He walked over to the glass container, picked up a piece of brown paper, and asked, "How many would you like?"

"Just one, please," she answered, her eyes not straying from the licorice.

As he reached in to remove a piece of the candy from the large stack, Nicholas spoke up. "We will take all the licorice."

The worker's hand stilled. "All, sir? There are over fifty pieces here."

Penelope placed her hand on Nicholas' sleeve. "That isn't necessary. I am perfectly happy with just one piece."

Placing his hand over hers, he said, "I saw the way your eyes lit up when you saw the licorice. Kindly allow me to do this for you."

"Thank you, Nicholas," she replied, hoping her words conveyed her gratitude for his touching gesture.

His eyes lingered on her face for a moment, and then he turned back towards the worker. "We will take three pieces now. Wrap up the rest and have them delivered to Hereford Hall on Grosvenor Street."

The clerk's eyes widened. "Yes, your grace." He quickly reached in and removed three pieces of the braided treat, extending it towards them.

Nicholas accepted the licorice and handed one to Penelope. When she took her first bite, she closed her eyes and chewed the treat with pleasure.

"This is brilliant." Penelope opened her eyes and realized that the duke was watching her with a smile on his face. "You're smiling," she pointed out.

"I am." His smile grew. "You baffle me. How can something so miniscule bring you such joy?"

Holding up her licorice, she shared, "To me, this candy reminds me of a past that I long to remember."

His smiled dimmed, and his tone grew cynical. "You wish to remember that your parents died, leaving you alone?"

The duchess gasped. "Nicholas, that was uncalled for."

"No, it's all right," Penelope assured her. "Memories of my

parents are all that I have left. I see my mother's smile as I stare out into a field of poppy flowers, or I hear my father's laugh in the wind. They are everywhere, because they are in here," she said, pointing at her heart.

"That's balderdash," Nicholas huffed as he opened the door.

"I apologize, dear. Nicholas has no right to speak to you that way," the duchess whispered as they exited the store.

On the pavement, Penelope turned towards Mildred. "It is all right. Everyone deals with grief in their own way."

"I am not grieving…" Nicholas started to say before she heard someone shout over him, "Cousin!"

Penelope turned her head towards the noise and saw Baldwin striding towards her with a bright smile on his face.

"I thought that was you," he said, giving her a quick embrace. "What are you doing in London?"

"After I last saw you, I…"

Her voice stopped as Nicholas demanded, "Who exactly are you?"

Baldwin frowned at the duke. "I am Baldwin Ellis, the Viscount of Mountgarret, and cousin to Miss Penelope Foster." His eyes grew challenging. "And you are?"

"I am the Duke of Blackbourne," Nicholas replied in a commanding voice. "Miss Foster is my ward."

Rather than bow or defer to the duke, Baldwin gave him an annoyed look. "I see that you are finally taking your guardianship of my cousin seriously, your grace," he drawled.

"You will stay away from Miss Foster," the duke ordered. "Do I make myself clear?"

Baldwin took a step closer to Nicholas. "That is unacceptable. She is my cousin, and your family has kept her from our family for far too long."

"If you approach my ward again, I will have you arrested," Nicholas threatened with narrowed eyes.

Penelope reached for Nicholas' sleeve and pleaded, "Please, Nicholas. Don't do this."

"Nicholas?" Baldwin asked with a raised brow. "Exactly how close are you two?"

Nicholas brushed off her hand as his demeanor became rigid. "What are you insinuating, Mountgarret?"

"Nicholas," the duchess warned in a hushed voice, her eyes roaming the pavement. A small group of people were standing around, watching them. "Do you intend to cause a scene?"

Penelope decided to take control of the conversation. She directed her comment towards her cousin. "Call on me tomorrow at Hereford Hall, and I will explain everything," she said, ignoring Nicholas' adamant refusal. "Now, go."

Once Baldwin began walking off, she turned her attention towards Nicholas.

He pointed at Baldwin's retreating figure. "Your cousin is not allowed in my home."

She tilted her chin. "May I ask why?"

"No, you may not. Need I remind you that you are my ward?"

"You are being unreasonable," she replied, turning towards the duchess.

"Penelope…" he growled, gripping her arm. "You will not defy me on this."

She turned around to give him her full attention. "I heard you. If you will not allow Baldwin into Hereford Hall, then we will take a walk around the gardens."

"Absolutely not," he declared.

Her chin began to quiver as she attempted to keep control of her emotions. "You would truly deny me a visit from my own cousin?"

Placing a comforting arm around her shoulders, the duchess said, "I would hope that my son wouldn't be so callous as to refuse to let you see your cousin." Her words challenged Nicholas.

Nicholas looked between them, but his eyes showed no signs of softening. "I am. For now. You are not allowed to leave Hereford Hall, for any reason."

Penelope bit the inside of her lip to prevent herself from crying. She thought she had found a friend, an ally in the duke. But she was wrong.

What else was she wrong about?

❧ 8 ❧

NICHOLAS SLAMMED THE LEDGER CLOSED AND SAT BACK IN HIS seat. For the past three days, Penelope had refused to speak to him, to even acknowledge him. She broke her fast in his mother's bedchamber, didn't stray from the library, and ate dinner in her room. When he refused a tray to be sent up for her supper, Penelope did not relent and chose to go hungry for the evening, rather than join him for dinner. She was a stubborn, vexing thing.

Why did her anger affect him to such a degree? As a captain of a frigate, he was responsible for discipline and flogging, and he had never flinched from his course. Now his ward was causing him to question if he had made the correct decision with his refusal to see her cousin. Lord Mountgarret had come to call on three separate occasions but had been turned away each time by the gatekeeper.

"Lord Northampton is here to see you, your grace," his butler announced, breaking through his thoughts.

Before he could respond, Everett walked into the room with an annoying grin on his face. "I just secured tickets to the Theatre Royal at Haymarket tonight for us."

"I'm not going," Nicholas replied.

Reaching into his green jacket pocket, Everett pulled out four tickets and held them up. "Even to see Elizabeth Hornsby?" He waved the tickets in the air. "She hasn't performed since her retirement in 1811, and it is for one night only."

He had previously heard Mrs. Hornsby sing, and she had the voice of an angel. Yet, that did not sway him. "I have a headache." That was at least the partial truth. Penelope was constantly giving him a headache.

Everett gave him a look of disbelief. "You would deny your mother and Miss Foster a chance to hear Elizabeth Hornsby?"

Nicholas threaded his fingers together and placed them on the desk. "I am sure that my mother has heard her sing."

"What about Miss Foster?"

"Most likely not. However, she isn't speaking to me at the moment." He frowned.

"What did you do?" Everett asked in an accusing tone as he put the tickets in his pocket.

Nicholas ignored his friend's tone. "I ordered her to stay away from her cousin. When she refused my simple request, I had her kept indoors for her safety."

"When did Miss Foster see Lord Mountgarret?"

Nicholas unthreaded his hands and leaned back in his seat. "He approached her on the pavement when we went into town. I informed him that I would have him arrested if he spoke to Penelope ever again."

Everett walked over and sat down in a chair across from him. "To clarify, you are keeping Penelope as a prisoner."

"Not as a prisoner," he insisted. "I am just ensuring she is protected."

"By locking her inside your townhouse."

He narrowed his eyes. "She was going to defy my wishes."

Everett eyed him with concern. "By chance, did you explain to your ward why you wished her to stay away from her cousin?"

"Not necessary."

Everett took his fingers and pressed them to the bridge of his nose and sighed, loudly. "You are a bloody fool. You can't lock your ward away," he proclaimed. "She is not a part of your crew."

Nicholas rose from his seat and turned to look out his large window. "I am used to giving an order and having people follow it, without question. Life is much simpler that way."

"So, what's your plan?" his friend asked, dropping his hand to his lap. "Keep Penelope hidden all Season, so she doesn't ever see her cousin?"

He turned back towards Everett. "No. My solicitor has already started an investigation into Lord Mountgarret. The Bow Street Runners will discover if he has any nefarious intentions."

"And if he doesn't?"

Nicholas clasped his hands behind his back. "There is a reason my uncle kept Penelope away from her family. I intend to do the same. After all, Lord Mountgarret may be a scoundrel, just as his father was."

"Your uncle was an egotistical, pompous man that only cared for himself," Everett pointed out, frowning.

Nicholas was silent for a moment, knowing Everett spoke the truth. "Regardless, I am Penelope's guardian, and I am responsible for her welfare."

"By locking her up?" his friend demanded. "That's your plan, to treat her the same way your uncle and father did?"

"I am nothing like them!" he shouted.

"No?" Everett said, jumping up from his seat. "I see it quite differently." He removed three tickets from his jacket pocket. "Apologize to Penelope. Take her to the opera tonight." He slammed the tickets onto the desk. "Be her champion, Nicholas, not her jailer."

Nicholas glanced down at the tickets. "I have done nothing to apologize for. I am merely ensuring that Penelope stays safe."

"I see," Everett replied, tapping the tickets with his finger.

"Don't you suppose that your ward will rebel against your hardened stance?"

"No. My staff is under strict instructions to keep her inside at all times."

Everett's lips quirked. "Then you don't know Penelope at all." He stepped back from the desk. "I hope to see you at the Theatre Royal tonight."

Glancing down at the tickets, Nicholas knew he had to make a choice. He could continue keeping her locked away at his estate, where they both were miserable, or he could take Penelope to the opera and spend a few hours with her in close proximity. His gesture might even sway him back into favor with her.

"Perhaps I can convince Penelope to go to the performance," he said, optimistically. "She might enjoy a night out."

Everett tipped his head towards the window. "Your ward has escaped." His voice was full of merriment.

Nicholas turned to look out the window and saw Penelope running towards the stables. "What the blazes! She wasn't supposed to leave the estate."

Everett chuckled. "I find Penelope to be quite entertaining."

Ignoring his gloating friend, Nicholas stormed out of his office. "Hawkins!"

His butler rounded the corner. "Yes, your grace?"

"I saw Miss Foster approaching the stables. Did you allow her to leave the estate?"

"Of course not, your grace," Hawkins replied in a tone that caused him to have serious doubt.

Nicholas walked over to the main door and threw it open. Why was being a guardian to an eighteen-year-old girl harder than commanding a whole crew during a time of war?

Penelope started brushing down Mildred. Nicholas made her so incredibly angry! He bestowed kindness one moment and then became hard-headed the next. Just when she thought he was softening towards her, Nicholas would block her out again. Infuriating man!

What right did he have to keep her away from her cousin? Baldwin was her family. She had grown up with him, and despite their four-year age difference, they were thick as thieves as children. When he had left for Eton, she had been devastated, but when he returned for holiday, it was as if they were never apart.

Her guardian had no idea what she was capable of. It was an easy thing to sneak out of her window and scale down the brick wall. It was a skill that she had mastered at the finishing school. While hiding out in her room, Penelope came to the realization that the duke might go back on his word and force her to marry a man of his choosing. She would need to come up with a plan in case she was forced to flee from Hereford Halls.

At least she had an ally in the duchess. Thank heavens for her. She was a kind, remarkable woman that showered love upon her.

Her thoughts were disturbed by the grizzly voice of her guardian. "Penelope."

Ignoring him, she kept brushing down her horse.

"Penelope," he repeated, his voice taking on a hardened edge. "You were under strict orders to stay inside Hereford Halls."

"I will not apologize for sneaking out," she said, not bothering to look in his direction. "It was unfair and cruel of you to demand such a thing."

From the corner of her eye, she saw him place his forearms on top of the stall. "It was within my rights."

She lowered the brush to her side before she turned towards Nicholas. "You have no right to keep me from my cousin by locking me away in your estate."

Nicholas wore a stern expression. "Your cousin is not to be trusted."

Her mouth gaped. "If I can't trust my cousin, then who can I trust?"

"I have opened an investigation into Lord Mountgarret—" Nicholas started.

"You are unbelievable," she spoke over him.

To her surprise, he gave her a look mixed with pity and frustration. "Not everyone is who they seem. Your cousin may very well be trying to steal your fortune."

Her eyes filled with tears. "I feel bad for you. You have locked your emotions away and have become so jaded that you refuse to feel anything." She swiped at a tear that rolled down her cheek. "You will not drag me down to your level, your grace."

He blinked, and then blinked again. "I am sorry you feel that way, but you are my charge. And if need be, I will protect you from yourself."

"Myself?" she found herself asking in disbelief.

"Had you considered that Lord Mountgarret may attempt to abduct you and force you to marry him?"

"Your insinuation is insulting. He is my cousin."

"It is not unheard of," the duke contended. "If the investigation yields nothing, then I will allow your cousin to call on you, under supervision, of course."

Penelope turned back towards her horse as she felt her anger rising. "Is there anything else?" she asked dismissively.

Silence settled between them for a moment.

"Do you intend to go riding?" he finally asked.

"Yes," she replied, seeing no reason to lie.

Nicholas shifted in his stance, and his boots crunched the dry straw on the ground. "Would you like me to escort you?"

"No."

Penelope could practically hear the displeasure radiating off his person. Rather than the rebuke that she had been expecting, he surprised her by saying, "I will go find two grooms to escort you."

"Thank you," she murmured as she resumed brushing her horse.

"I have asked Mr. Pratt to call upon you tomorrow to discuss the status of your company," the duke revealed.

Her hand stilled, but she kept her rigid back towards him. "That was most kind of you."

Nicholas cleared his throat, and if she had to guess, sounded nervous. "Everett secured tickets to see Elizabeth Hornsby at the Theatre Royal at Haymarket this evening. Would you care to go?"

"Just us?" she asked, unsure of how she felt about that.

"He was able to obtain three tickets. My mother will be joining us as well."

Penelope was torn. As much as she wanted to avoid Nicholas, she had always had a desire to hear Elizabeth Hornsby sing.

"I would like that very much," she found herself saying over her shoulder.

"Good," he said, stepping back. "Until this evening, then."

She watched as he walked towards Mr. Grant, the lead groom. How did Nicholas do that? When she had stepped into the stable, she was at odds with the duke, but then after one conversation, she found herself agreeing to attend a performance with him.

Why did Nicholas have to be so blasted handsome? If he was unfortunate looking, then she would have no issue with turning him down. However, one look into his dark brown eyes, and she found herself doing his bidding.

Perhaps she did need help from herself. After all, if her resolve could be swayed so easily by the duke, then maybe she was in trouble after all.

❧ 9 ❧

PENELOPE SMILED AS SHE HURRIED UP THE FRONT STEPS OF Hereford Hall. Riding always gave her a welcome respite from her burdens. Her hair had begun falling out of the tight chignon she'd been wearing, and she tucked it behind her ears.

The door opened, and Mr. Hawkins greeted her cheerfully. "You are looking well, Miss Foster."

"Thank you," she murmured, walking into the entrance hall. "Riding has always been one of my favorite pastimes." She glanced around the room before she lowered her voice. "His grace saw me escape. I hope I did not get you into too much trouble. I know you were tasked with ensuring I did not leave the townhouse."

Mr. Hawkins shook his head. "Not at all, Miss. However, I would much rather have you escape through the servant's entrance than scaling down the side of the building."

Her lips twitched in amusement. "Where's the fun in that?"

"At least you wouldn't risk breaking your neck," the butler replied with a huff.

"True," she agreed. "However, the safe choice isn't always

the right choice." Without saying another word, she headed towards the main stairs and hurried up the steps.

At the top of the landing, she was met by her lady's maid. "We must hurry if we want to prepare you for the performance tonight."

"Do I have time for a bath?" Penelope asked, hopefully.

Claire nodded. "The bath was already prepared, but I cannot verify how warm the water is now. Your ride took longer than I anticipated."

She followed Claire towards her room. "I had a lot on my mind."

Claire opened her door and stood aside for her to enter. The metal bath was sitting next to the fireplace, and a towel was draped on a chair next to the tub. After Claire helped her undress, Penelope slipped into the tepid water.

After a quick soak, Claire opened the door and walked back into the room holding one of her elaborate gowns. "It's time to dress you and style your hair," she announced as she placed the dress onto her bed.

Penelope rose from the bath, accepted the towel from Claire and began to dry herself off. Then they started the arduous process of dressing her for the evening. Once her gown was buttoned up, she sat down at the dressing table.

A knock came at her door before it was pushed open. The duchess walked into the room. She wore an exquisite maroon colored gown, with pearls hanging low around her neck. She smiled kindly. "Penelope, your dress is gorgeous."

Penelope glanced down at her white gown, with puffy sleeves, a round neckline, and pink embroidered flowers on the net overlay. "It is a beautiful gown, isn't it?"

Mildred walked closer to her and said, "I have brought you something to wear tonight." She extended a diamond-encrusted pendant necklace. "My mother allowed me to wear this necklace the first time I made an appearance in Society."

"I don't dare," Penelope whispered as she tentatively reached out and fingered the glittering diamonds.

"Pish-posh," the duchess disagreed, placing it around her neck. "I know for a fact that you do not have any jewelry with you. It is merely my duty to loan you some of mine for the time being."

Looking into the mirror, she met Mildred's gaze as she acknowledged the gesture. "Thank you. You have been most kind to me."

The duchess' eyes filled with moisture as she stepped to the side so Claire could finish styling her hair. "It's my privilege. I always wanted a girl to spoil." She blinked her tears away before adding, "Tonight is your first social engagement. You will receive curious glances, but do not give them any heed. Keep your head held high and a smile on your lips. It will drive the gentlemen mad."

"I'm surprised Nicholas is letting me attend the Theatre Royal tonight," Penelope said as Claire started weaving pink flowers into her elaborate hairstyle.

Mildred clasped her hands in front of her. "Have patience with him. He is struggling."

"Struggling?" Penelope repeated back. There were many words she would use to describe Nicholas... arrogant, confident, argumentative... but 'struggling' was not one of them.

Furrowing her brow, the duchess lowered her voice. "He feels incredible guilt over the death of his brother, Alfred," she admitted.

Curious, Penelope asked, "How did Alfred die?"

A sorrowful look came over Mildred's face. "In a horrible accident." She took a moment to compose herself before sharing, "Sometimes I think I lost both of my boys that day."

Claire stepped back and excused herself from the room.

"In what way?" Penelope asked.

The crinkle lines around the duchess' eyes look tired.

"Nicholas never recovered from Alfred's death. I see the anger in his eyes, and I can hear the regret in his voice. The only time I have seen him smile is when he looks at you."

Penelope let out a disbelieving huff. "You must be mistaken. I am a burden to your son, nothing more."

A tentative smile came to the duchess' lips. "You're wrong. You are more than just my son's ward. You are giving him a renewed purpose."

Penelope rose and walked over to the bed where Claire had laid out her matching kid gloves. "Nicholas and I do not see eye to eye. He views me as an unruly child needing protection."

"He is fiercely protective of those under his command, and he takes his role as your guardian seriously."

"I am eighteen," Penelope remarked, pulling one glove on. "I should be able to make my own choices."

"Be careful what you wish for," the duchess stated. "I have found it's a lot easier if you have someone to help you along the way."

"Nicholas frustrates me. One moment he is kind, and the other he becomes cantankerous."

The duchess caught her off guard by asking, "Which side of Nicholas do you believe is the real him?"

Penelope hesitated. She couldn't answer that question, because she honestly didn't know.

The duchess took pity on her and opened the door. "Come. We will finish our conversation later."

Penelope had just begun to descend the stairs when she saw a sharply-dressed Nicholas walking into the entry hall. He looked up at her, and she saw his eyes grow wide. In them, she saw approval, making her feel desirable. She expected him to turn away or blink his emotions away as he usually did, but instead, he maintained his gaze.

When she stopped in front of him, Nicholas reached down and brought her hand to his lips. "You look beautiful, Penelope."

"Thank you," she replied, pleased that she had found her voice.

Having Nicholas look at her in that way greatly unnerved her. His anger she could handle, but longing was something entirely different. Perhaps she imagined it. Yes, of course. It was all in her imagination.

Nicholas hated going to the theatre. He despised the crowds, and the whispers that accompanied him wherever he went. Fortunately, no one dared approach him or even attempted to maintain his gaze, for he was feared, respected, and infamous. The stories of his naval victories had been shared and embellished by the ton. But despite all his accomplishments and accolades, there were still some members of the peerage that didn't believe he deserved the title of Duke of Blackbourne. And he was one of them.

Escorting his mother and Penelope into the Theatre Royal, Nicholas was not surprised when all eyes turned towards them, the room growing silent. Only no one was staring at him or the duchess. They were all watching his ward, who seemed oblivious to the attention. Her eyes were filled with wonder as they darted around the finely decorated entrance foyer with the grand staircase leading up to the next level.

He was leading them towards the staircase when he saw Everett approach them from across the foyer. "You came," his friend said with a welcoming smile. "I had almost given up hope."

Nicholas stopped, and Penelope removed her hand from his arm. To his surprise, he immediately felt the loss of contact.

Penelope dropped into a curtsy. "Lord Northampton, it is a pleasure to see you."

Everett bowed. "Likewise, Miss Foster." He leaned closer and joked, "I would have preferred it if you had worn your orange gown this evening."

Penelope let out a bark of laughter, drawing attention from the other patrons, and she quickly brought her gloved hand up to cover her mouth. Nicholas watched her cheeks grow pink and knew she was embarrassed by the volume of her laughter.

He leaned closer to her and whispered reassuringly, "I personally would have preferred the spectacles."

She kept her voice low, the vulnerability laced in her words. "I'm afraid I ruined my first impression."

Nicholas reached out and placed his hand on her elbow. "Not in the least. Besides, you are by far the most beautiful woman in the room."

The corner of her lips twitched as she replied, "Flattery? Really, your grace. I thought we decided not to use flowery words with each other."

"If you recall, I said that 'flattery has its limitations and doesn't work on me'," he teased, enjoying their personal interlude. "All gentlemen have flattery in their arsenal."

Everett cleared his throat, bringing both of their gazes back towards him. "Your grace, may I suggest if you would like to continue this private conversation that you do so away from prying eyes."

"What a marvelous idea, Lord Northampton. I can't wait to see our private box," his mother answered for them, looping her arm through Penelope's and leading her up the stairs.

Trailing behind his ward, Nicholas saw that Everett kept giving him side glances. "What?" he demanded.

"Would you like to explain that interaction with Miss Foster just now?"

"No."

"It appeared that you were flirting with the girl," Everett pointed out with mirth in his voice.

Nicholas clenched his jaw, refusing to dignify his words with a response. He was not flirting with Penelope. He was stating a simple fact. She was the most beautiful girl in the room. There was no denying that.

Not taking the hint, Everett continued. "I thought she wasn't speaking to you."

"I didn't apologize, if that is what you are asking," he stated, watching Penelope's hips sway back and forth in the most enticing fashion.

Tugging on the sleeves of his dress shirt, Everett appeared unperturbed by his annoyed tone. "Of course not, your grace. Apologizing to a woman is beneath you."

"Rather than apologize, I explained why I wanted her to stay away from her cousin," he said, ignoring his friend's back-handed remark.

"How did she take that?"

"Not well," he admitted.

"Have you heard anything regarding the investigation?"

Nicholas shook his head. "Not yet, but I hope to soon."

"For your sake, I hope so." Everett increased his stride to catch up with the ladies and led them to their private box.

Once they were situated in their seats, Nicholas watched Penelope in fascination. She wore the same look of wonder that she had when she first walked into the theatre. He had never enjoyed the theatre as much as he did with his ward. She forced him to take a closer look at his surroundings.

When Mrs. Elizabeth Hornsby took the stage, his eyes strayed back towards Penelope. He didn't think he would ever tire of watching her. The pure innocence of her captivated him.

Suddenly, the room erupted in cheers and everyone rose from their seats. Nicholas realized that he had been staring at Penelope for so long that it was now intermission. Once his ward returned to her seat, he asked, "Have you enjoyed the performance so far?"

"Oh, yes," she gushed. "Mrs. Hornsby's voice is exquisite."

"It is," he agreed.

A few knocks came at the door, and Everett started chuckling. "It is time for me to send Penelope's admirers away." He rose and walked over to the door. "This evening keeps getting better and better."

Nicholas watched as Penelope smoothed out her gown, appearing nervous. He had no intention of introducing her to any members of the ton tonight, especially any gentlemen.

"You have no reason to be nervous," he assured her. "We are just here to listen to the performance."

Penelope nodded gratefully at him. "Thank you..." Her words stopped when her cousin pushed through the door, despite Everett ordering him to stop.

"Baldwin," she said, rising from her seat.

Nicholas jumped up and stepped in front of her. "I thought I told you to stay away from Miss Foster."

Baldwin's eyes narrowed as he stepped closer to him. "Penelope is my cousin, and I refuse to stay away from her. You have no right to keep her from me."

"It wasn't a request," he growled.

"Your grace, please," Penelope said from behind him. "He is my cousin."

Not backing down, Nicholas declared, "As I explained earlier, family can't always be trusted."

Baldwin scoffed. "You would know that first hand, wouldn't you, your grace?"

"What exactly is that supposed to mean?" he asked, clenching his fists into balls.

Baldwin took a step closer and now their faces were only inches apart. "Family can always be disposed of," the viscount stated dryly.

Nicholas brought back his fist and punched Lord Mountgarret in the jaw, knocking him to the ground. "Get out! If I ever see you again, I will do more than have you arrested."

"Baldwin!" Penelope shouted as she came from behind him and rushed over to her cousin on the floor. She knelt beside Baldwin and turned her furious gaze up towards him. "Why did you hit him?"

"Step away from Lord Mountgarret," he ordered.

Penelope opened her mouth to protest when her cousin propped himself up and whispered something in her ear. Her skin paled as her eyes shot up to meet his.

She knew his secret.

10

NICHOLAS REVIEWED THE SAME LEDGER THREE TIMES BEFORE HE slammed it shut. He couldn't seem to get Penelope's look of horror at the theatre out of his mind. After Baldwin exited the box, his mother suggested they leave before the next act.

He had offered his arm to Penelope, but she had refused his assistance. They'd ridden in awkward silence all the way back to Hereford Halls. The evening had been a disaster. Regardless, he would not apologize for his behavior. His job was to ensure his charge was protected, and Baldwin was a direct threat to her.

Why couldn't Penelope see that? He sighed as he ran his hand through his hair. And now she knew his secret. He had killed his own brother. She would never forgive him for that. Why should she? He had never forgiven himself.

He rose from the seat at his desk and turned towards the window. Trees and lush green fields surrounded his estate on the north side of his property, and the south side butted against the bustling streets of London.

Nicholas missed the expansive ocean, the sound of the water breaking against the hull of his ship, and the cry of an occasional

LAURA BEERS

seagull. He should be happy as a duke, but his heart mourned for what he had lost. His brother, his crew, and his ship.

"Your grace," Mr. Hawkins said from the doorway, "Mr. Fulton is here to see you."

"Send him in," he responded, his gaze not wavering from the window.

He heard Mr. Fulton walk into the room. "Your grace, the Bow Street Runners have given me their preliminary report of Lord Mountgarret."

Now his solicitor had his attention. "And?" he asked, turning around.

Mr. Fulton removed papers from a file. "Lord Mountgarret is heavily in debt. His estate in Cardiff is entailed or it would have already been repossessed. He keeps a minimal staff at his estate and is renting an apartment at Albany on Piccadilly street during the Season."

Nicholas sat down on his chair and replied, "It's not uncommon for a fashionable bachelor to rent an apartment at Albany. Besides reducing his need for a staff, it allows gentlemen to be close to the clubs and shops of St. James, as well as the Houses of Parliament."

Extending a paper over the desk, his solicitor stated, "Lord Mountgarret can barely afford the rent for his apartment, much less pay for entertainment. The Bow Street Runners discreetly followed him and discovered he spends almost all his time at the House of Lords. Surprisingly enough, he rarely indulges in the vices that are typically associated with bachelors."

Nicholas took a moment to scan the paper which showed Baldwin's movements for the past week. "Was anything else discovered?"

Mr. Fulton nodded, causing his double chin to swish about. "When Lord Mountgarret did attend a ball or social gathering, he was always spotted with an heiress or a debutante with a large dowry."

98

Crinkling the paper in his hand, Nicholas proclaimed, "I knew it. He's a fortune hunter."

"That he is, your grace," Mr. Fulton concluded. "If the viscount does not marry, and soon, then he most likely will be tossed into debtor's prison."

Nicholas grimaced, knowing that Miss Foster would not be easily convinced that her dear cousin saw her only as a means to an end. "How much is he in debt?"

Mr. Fulton reached into the file and shuffled through a few pages before revealing, "About £50,000."

"How did he acquire this debt?"

Lowering the papers to his lap, his solicitor said, "He inherited it."

"All of it?"

"Aye. His father took out many loans before his death, but his investments never panned out, leaving his son to sort out his mess," his solicitor shared. "Lord Mountgarret inherited his title when he was barely eighteen and has worked hard to make a dent in the compounding debt. By all accounts, he appears to be frugal with his funds, but it's not enough. His estate brings in only £75 a year and is in desperate need of repair."

"And the viscount doesn't gamble?" Nicholas asked, leaning back in his seat.

"The Bow Street Runner assigned to follow him said he stayed far away from the known gambling dens," his solicitor stated. "He also spent minimal time at White's and never placed any bets in the book."

Frowning, he asked, "What else was discovered?"

The solicitor extended a stack of papers to him. "The viscount has no other relations, other than Miss Foster, of course, and he is an active member of the House of Lords. There is even talk of him running for Prime Minister one day."

Nicolas leaned forward and accepted the papers. "A wealthy wife would solve all of his problems," he commented.

"That it would, your grace," his solicitor confirmed.

"I will review these later," he said, placing the pages down. "Thank you for arriving early for the meeting with Mr. Pratt."

Mr. Fulton rested his elbow on his arm chair. "I wouldn't miss it. I have been attempting to schedule a meeting with Mr. Pratt for some time now. He has yet to respond to my missives."

A knock came at the door. "Enter," he ordered.

Mr. Hawkins opened the door and announced, "Mr. Joseph Pratt and Mr. Dudley Pratt have arrived for your meeting, your grace."

"Thank you, Hawkins," he said, rising. "Please inform Miss Foster that her presence is requested in my office."

Mr. Fulton gave him a puzzled look. "Is it wise to include Miss Foster in our meeting?"

"I believe Miss Foster would be interested in our conversation, considering it is *her* company that we will be discussing," Nicholas replied in a dry tone.

Rising from his chair, his solicitor's face turned expressionless. "As you wish, your grace."

As Nicholas came around the desk, he asserted, "Miss Foster is my charge, and I intend to ensure she fully understands the magnitude of her portfolio. I hope that you are on board for this assignment."

"I am," Mr. Fulton responded quickly.

He nodded his acknowledgement as he walked over to the drink tray. He understood his solicitor's reluctance to include Penelope in their meeting, but she was not like most women he had associated with over the years. She was clever, and he had no doubt that she would easily grasp the complexity of her investments.

Regardless, it would give him a chance to speak with her again. Even if only for a moment.

Sitting on a chaise lounge, Penelope had just turned a page in her book when she saw Mr. Hawkins walk into the library. He stopped by the door and announced, "His grace has requested your presence in his study."

"Inform his grace that I am busy at the moment," she replied, returning her attention back to her book.

The butler walked further into the room. "Normally I would be happy to relay the message, but Mr. Joseph Pratt, Mr. Dudley Pratt, and Mr. Fulton are all assembled there."

"In that case," she murmured, placing her book down on a side table, "I believe I shall join them."

A smile came to Mr. Hawkins's lips. "As you wish, Miss Foster."

Penelope hurried down the hall and stopped at the mirror near Nicholas' study. She would be lying to herself if she didn't admit she felt flustered about seeing the duke again. Last night had started off promising but had ended with Nicholas engaging in fisticuffs with her cousin. What had he been thinking? For someone who relied so much on order, she was surprised by the chaos that he had caused.

She took a moment to gather her courage. Nicholas had arranged this meeting so she could further understand the status of her company. Forcing a smile to her lips, she walked through the open door of the study, and her treacherous eyes sought out Nicholas next to the window.

When Nicholas saw her, his eyes lit up, and he quickly approached her. "Miss Foster, thank you for joining us." He leaned closer and whispered, "We need to put our differences aside at the moment and work as a united front."

Penelope nodded her understanding as he stepped back.

"Thank you for including me, your grace." She turned her attention towards the solicitor. "It is good to see you again, Mr. Fulton."

He bowed. "You are looking well, Miss Foster."

She smiled demurely at him as Nicholas proceeded to introduce her to the two other gentlemen. "This is Mr. Joseph Pratt," he said, pointing towards a nicely-dressed older gentlemen with silver hair, sharp features, and crinkle lines around his eyes.

Mr. Pratt stepped forward, his eyes reflecting kindness. "You may not remember me, but I watched you grow up from the time you were a little babe." He smiled fondly at her. "You look just like your mother," he paused, "but you have your father's smile."

Penelope searched his face, but she could not recall meeting this man. "I apologize…"

Mr. Pratt held up his hand. "You have no reason to apologize. You were still young the last time I saw you." He turned his hand back towards the younger gentleman. A very handsome gentleman. "I would like to introduce you to my son, Mr. Dudley Pratt. He has been helping me run the Foster Company since your father passed."

Dudley stepped forward and bowed respectfully. "It is an honor to meet you, Miss Foster."

In response, she curtsied and took a moment to admire the man in front of her. He was tall, with broad shoulders, and had the same sharp facial features as his father. His eyes reflected both intelligence and compassion.

Nicholas' hand came to her elbow as he escorted her towards the sofa. Once she was situated, he sat down next to her, and the rest of the men sat opposite them.

The duke spoke up. "Miss Foster has expressed an interest in learning more about her company and all of its investments."

Joseph smiled indulgently at her. "That's not necessary. Your father left his company in my capable hands, and we have nearly doubled the profits over the past few years."

"Be that as it may," she started, "I would like to take a more active role in my company."

Leaning forward in his seat, Dudley stated, "I think that is a fine idea. Your father worked hard to build up his dynasty, and you have every right to continue its legacy."

"Thank you," she responded.

"Allow me to tell you a little about your company," the older gentleman began, smiling at her. "At the Foster Company, we specialize in finding the impossible. We secure the finest silk, wine, brandy, linen, lace, fine cambrics, and many other commodities. We have amassed a fleet of ships to go all over the world, making the Foster Company one of the most profitable companies in all of Britain."

"What exactly does Foster export?" she asked.

"Anything and everything," Joseph replied. "Which is why, my dear, you are a very wealthy woman."

Penelope nodded. "Where are your offices located?"

"We maintain our offices in London, but there are two large warehouses by the docks," the younger man explained. "If you would like, I would be happy to take you on a tour."

"I would like that very much," she assured him. "I have every intention of being involved in my company from here on out."

Joseph's wrinkled brow lifted. "Surely, you jest. After all, a young woman of your station has much more pressing matters than learning about trade."

"Which are, Mr. Pratt?" she questioned in a wry tone.

His eyes darted towards Nicholas as if to ask if she was a simpleton. "Balls, soirees, house parties, shopping… things of that nature."

Penelope felt her composure and confidence beginning to slip. Clearly, Mr. Joseph Pratt did not take her seriously, and his rejection stung. Perhaps he was right. She was only eighteen, and she had no knowledge of business dealings.

She shifted her gaze towards Nicholas, hoping he would tell her what to do. Instead, he gave her a look of encouragement, one that caused her to strengthen her resolve. She could do this.

"I find I have ample time on my hands to learn the business dealings of the Foster Company and attend social gatherings," she stated in a firm voice. "I wish to be consulted on all aspects of my company from here on out."

With disapproval on his features, Joseph regarded her for a long moment before saying, "I believe that is unwise. Women cannot possibly grasp business, and I do not have time to cater to your every whim. I have a company to run."

Pressing her lips together, she opened her mouth to voice her displeasure, but Nicholas spoke first. "As Miss Foster's guardian, I have the authority to hire and fire anyone at the Foster Company. Miss Foster is a confident, clever woman, and she desires to take her place at the head of her company, at least for the time being. Anyone that does not support her decision, will be terminated, *immediately*." He lifted his brow at Mr. Joseph Pratt. "What will it be, Mr. Pratt?"

The older man offered her a forced smile. "We would be honored to work with you at your company, Miss Foster."

Penelope glanced over and saw Dudley attempting to hide a smile behind his gloved hand. He caught her gaze and lowered his hand. "Would you prefer a tour of the warehouses or offices first?"

"Warehouses," she responded with enthusiasm.

He tipped his head at her. "So be it. Would tomorrow afternoon fit your schedule?"

She glanced over at Nicholas, and he gave her a brief nod. "Yes, it would."

"Excellent," Mr. Dudley Pratt said, rising from his seat. "I look forward to it."

Penelope rose and watched as Mr. Joseph Pratt and his son left the study. She turned her gaze back towards Mr. Fulton.

"Would it be possible for you to review all the records of the Foster Company?"

"Do you suspect an issue?" the solicitor asked with a frown.

She shook her head. "No, but it is best to be cautious."

"Smart move," Mr. Fulton replied. "I will request the records be sent over, and I will have a complete audit performed."

"When you have received the records, would you also mind explaining them to me?" she asked.

Mr. Fulton gave her a reassuring smile. "Of course, Miss Foster." The solicitor bowed and left the room.

Penelope turned back towards Nicholas and noticed that he was watching her. "You did well," he said.

She let out a disbelieving huff. "I daresay that was not the case." She ran her fingers along the side of the sofa. "Thank you for stepping in when you did."

"I merely reminded Mr. Pratt of his place."

She shook her head, causing her ringlets to sway back and forth. "It was more than that," she acknowledged. "You stood up for me."

Nicholas' face grew serious as he replied, "Why would I not? You are capable of great things, Penelope. Don't let anyone else convince you otherwise."

She held his gaze, and even though no words were spoken, none were necessary. To him, it was a small thing to defend her. But to her, it meant everything.

11

PENELOPE'S EYES ROAMED OVER THE SHELVES IN THE DUKE'S library as she looked for any book that piqued her interest. There were so many books available for her to read. Normally the duchess would adjourn to the library with her after dinner, but she said she didn't feel well this evening and retired early.

As she stood on her tip-toes to reach for a book, she heard someone walk in, but she didn't need to turn around to know who it was. She already knew. Nicholas. Every time he walked into a room now, she could feel his presence.

The steps came closer. "Allow me to help you, Penelope." He easily reached up and pulled out the book that she'd been reaching for.

"Thank you," she murmured as he handed it to her.

Rather than stepping back, he remained close, and she smelled the familiar scent of leather and musk, which was quickly becoming her favorite smell.

"I've been hoping to speak to you alone," he said, his voice sounding less confident than before.

"About?"

He brought his brows together as he shifted his gaze over her shoulder. "What Lord Mountgarret whispered to you last night."

She gave him a quizzical look. "Did you overhear what he said?"

"No," he replied, bringing his gaze back to hers. "I just saw the way your face paled, and I assumed it was about me killing my brother."

Penelope heard the anguish in his words, confirming what she already knew in her heart. Nicholas was not a murderer.

"Do you expect me to believe you killed your own brother?"

He stepped back and nodded. "My actions did."

Reaching out, Penelope took his hand. "I know you didn't kill your brother, regardless of what you are saying."

Nicholas looked down at their entwined hands before bringing his sad gaze back up to her. "You are wrong. My brother is dead because of me."

"Come," she said, leading him towards the sofa. "Will you tell me what happened?"

Once they were seated, Nicholas dropped her hand and balled his into tight fists. "Eight years ago, Alfred and I came home to Lawrence Abbey for a holiday from Cambridge. We decided to go riding to the medieval ruins on our property." He hesitated, clenching his jaw. "Growing up, my parents had strictly forbidden us from going to the ruins, but we were older now, more mature. We didn't heed their advice."

Nicholas leaned forward and placed his elbows on his legs. "It had drizzled that morning and the stone was slick, but we still went exploring. As we walked up the dilapidated staircase towards the second level, the wood gave way, and we crashed down to the floor below us." He jumped up from his seat and strode over to the fireplace.

After a long drawn out silence, Penelope rose and walked over to him. "Is that how your brother died?"

He cleared his throat, and the shakiness in his voice was

unmistakable. "When my brother and I fell, I landed on top of him. He broke my fall, allowing me to survive." He placed his hands onto the mantle and leaned in. "It took me hours to climb out of the wreckage to seek help, but by then it was too late."

"That sounds like a horrible accident," she stated.

Nicholas let out a choked laugh before responding, "Many people of the ton found his death suspicious, but my father refused to open an investigation, claiming our family had been through enough." He frowned. "Unfortunately, the rumors escalated, and everywhere I went I heard the whispers and saw the stares."

"People can be cruel…"

He spoke over her. "I deserved it. I deserved all of it!" he shouted, loudly. "It is because of me that my brother is dead."

Penelope stayed rooted in her spot, despite his aggressive tone. She could hear the tremble of pain in his voice. He was hurting with such intensity that she could feel his sadness, his pain.

"No. Your brother died because of an unfortunate accident. It was not your fault."

"It was!" He turned his red-rimmed eyes up towards the ceiling. "If we had stayed away from the ruins as we were directed, then none of this would have happened. The rule was in place for a reason."

Suddenly, it was becoming increasingly clear why Nicholas was so insistent on her following rules and behaving a certain way. His brother had died when they broke a rule.

"Is that why you joined the Royal Navy?"

His expression was twisted with anguish as he admitted, "My father couldn't stand the sight of me. I suspect that he believed the rumors that I killed my own brother so that I would be in line to become a duke. At the time, my uncle had no children, and my father was the heir-apparent." He sighed. "Which is why I decided to leave. I bought a commission in the Royal Navy, and I left without saying good-bye."

"Not even to your mother?"

A flicker of guilt flashed in his eyes. "She blames me as well."

Penelope didn't believe that for one moment and decided to ask, "Have you ever asked her?"

He shook his head. "I didn't need to. I see it in the way she looks at me."

"Your mother loves you," she asserted as she took a step closer to him. "She is grieving your loss as well."

"You don't know what you are talking about," he replied dismissively.

Nicholas started to turn, but she put her hand on his sleeve, stopping him. "I do. Just as I can tell that you are hurting." She took a small step forward. "You are a good man, and you did not cause your brother's death. It was just an accident."

"How would you know?" he asked in defiance.

"Because, Nicholas," she began, hoping her eyes conveyed her heart-felt feelings, "you are many things, but you are not a murderer. It's time for you to stop blaming yourself and start to forgive yourself."

"Penelope… I can't," he insisted. "You think you know me, but you don't. I am not the man you think I am."

"You're right," she confirmed as she brought her hand up to his cheek. "You're better."

Penelope saw it in his eyes. The anguish, the frustration. He didn't believe her.

"I am not worthy of your praise," he said with a hushed, pained tone.

"You are hiding your heart behind a facade because you are afraid you don't deserve happiness," she remarked. "But you do. You deserve to be happy."

"How can I be happy when Alfred is dead?"

Penelope lowered her hand from his cheek, understanding his

turmoil all too well. "When my parents died, I felt so alone. So empty. All I remember is that Baldwin tried to cheer me up after we received word that my parents perished in that boating accident." She swallowed slowly as she admitted, "I even wished that I had been on that boat with them. It would have been so much simpler."

"Oh, Penelope," Nicholas murmured, his eyes full of compassion.

"Then, I was sent off to the finishing school, and I met my dear friends. I didn't feel as alone anymore," she shared. "While I grieved for my parents, I grieved the loss of my aunt and cousin as well. I wrote letters, but I never got a response. I later found out that Baldwin never received those letters, and he didn't even know where I was."

"How did you discover that?"

"After I returned home from finishing school, I rode towards the pond that divided my cousin's property from Brighton Hall. That's where I saw Baldwin for the first time in five years."

Nicholas frowned and she could see the suspicion creeping back into his eyes. "And he just happened to be there? Waiting for you?"

"No," Penelope insisted. "It was by chance. My aunt passed away a few months ago, and he had buried her at the family ancestral plot near the pond. He was visiting her when I rode up."

He wiped his hand over his chin thoughtfully. "Baldwin is not…" His voice drifted off as his eyes bored into hers.

"Is not what?" she prodded.

Nicholas hesitated, appearing to measure his words carefully. "Baldwin is telling the truth. My uncle didn't inform anyone of your location."

"I know," she said, turning away from Nicholas. "My cousin has never lied to me."

"Would you like to see him?" he blurted out.

Penelope spun back around. "I would, very much," she replied honestly.

Stepping back, his face grew expressionless. "Then I will arrange it."

A smile came to her face. "Thank you. Thank you so much," she gushed.

Penelope watched as his hand rose as if to touch her arm, but then he lowered it.

"Thank you for believing in me." His words were spoken reverently.

"You did the same for me when you stood up to Mr. Pratt," she declared, holding his gaze.

"I have no doubt that you can run the Foster Company, if you so desire," he said. "You continue to amaze me, Penelope."

Nicholas' words were spoken with such tenderness that her heart began to race, and she found herself taking a step closer to him. He stiffened, but he didn't move away.

"It's late," she murmured, feeling self-conscious about her bold actions. "I should retire."

He bowed. "Of course. Will you join me tomorrow for breakfast?"

"I'll be there," she assured him before turning to leave.

"Excellent," he said. "And… Penelope…"

She stilled. "Yes?"

"Thank you," he breathed, his eyes roaming her face.

"Anytime, your grace."

"No more 'your grace' for you," he insisted, taking a step closer. "I don't ever want to hear that from your lips again."

She nodded, unable to find her voice to speak even if she had known what to say.

Nicholas drew a deep, unsteady breath, as his piercing brown eyes gazed at her. Staring deep into his eyes, Penelope could see that his confidence had been stripped away, replaced by uncertainty. Was this the true Nicholas?

Her lips parted, and his eyes darted to her mouth, breaking the spell that had been cast over her. She mumbled a good night and swiftly left the library.

Racing down the hall, Penelope couldn't imagine what the duke must be thinking about her. She was his ward, his responsibility, and the last thing he needed was her swooning over him.

Nicholas had just placed the quill down next to the inkpot when Everett walked into his study. His friend tossed his top hat onto the sofa and dropped down next to it. "What a fine day it is."

"Why are you in such a good mood?" he asked, leaning back in his seat.

"Why would I not be?" Everett smiled. "Are you being a curmudgeon today?"

He waved his hand over all the paperwork on his desk. "How do you have any spare time with all the responsibility associated with your title?"

"Well, I only have a townhouse in London and a country estate near Bath," Everett said. "Plus, I am only a marquess."

"Would you like to be a duke?" he asked as he picked up a stack of papers and shuffled them before setting them aside.

His friend laughed. "If only it was that simple to relieve our burdens."

Nicholas rose and walked over to the drink tray. As he poured two drinks, he inquired, "Not that I am complaining, but what brings you by today?"

He walked over and handed a glass to Everett.

"I thought you might want to go riding."

"I am unavailable at the moment," Nicholas stated, bringing the glass up to his lips. "Perhaps later."

His friend raised his brow as he sat back in his seat. "Too busy to go riding and take a break from the drudgery of work?"

He opened his mouth to respond, but Mr. Hawkins walked into the room, announcing, "Your grace, Lord Mountgarret is here to see you."

"Send him in," he directed, ignoring Everett's blatant stare. He didn't have time to explain himself at the moment.

Lord Mountgarret walked into the room with a stern expression on his face. He bowed. "Your grace, thank you for agreeing to see me." He turned towards Everett and acknowledged him. "It is good to see you again, Lord Northampton."

Nicholas placed his glass down onto his desk and didn't bother to wait for Everett's response before addressing the viscount. "Let's be frank. You are only here because Penelope wishes to see you. If I had my way, you would never be able to even glance in her direction."

With a hardened look, Lord Mountgarret went to say something, but Nicholas put his hand up to stop his words. "My ward believes you to be an honorable man," he said.

"But you don't," the viscount remarked.

Nicholas eyed him for a moment. "Honestly, no."

"Your uncle took Penelope away from her only family. He robbed us of her for all those years," Lord Mountgarret stated. "My mother should have been her guardian."

"Yet, she wasn't," Nicholas contended. "Your father was a known gambler, and my uncle wanted to ensure Penelope, and her fortune, were protected."

"Clearly, you believe I take after my father," the viscount declared.

Nicholas shrugged. "Perhaps."

Lord Mountgarret took a step further into the room. "You

should know that I have gone to the magistrate," he informed him. "I plan to strip you of your guardianship over Penelope."

He scoffed. "On what grounds?"

"Everyone knows what you had to do to inherit the dukedom. It is in Penelope's best interest to steer clear of you and your reputation," the viscount spat out.

Nicholas noticed that Everett had placed his drink onto a side table, preparing for his next move. "You're wrong," he replied in a steely voice. "My brother died in a horrible accident, an accident that I relive every day, every moment, but it was just that… an accident." He leaned back onto the edge of his desk. "Penelope is home."

"Home?" Lord Mountgarret questioned in disbelief.

Realizing his blunder, Nicholas quickly corrected, "Penelope and I have come to an agreement that she will be allowed to pick her own suitor, assuming he is worthy of her. Furthermore, my mother has been tutoring her and has been taking her to social gatherings. Until she makes her selection, she will remain here at Hereford Hall with me."

"I understand that she is to have a ball in her honor," the viscount stated.

He nodded. "Yes. I will ensure that you receive an invitation."

"Thank you."

Nicholas placed his hands on the desk next to him and gripped the sides. "I am allowing you to see Penelope, but only supervised visits."

Lord Mountgarret wore a look of annoyance. "May I ask why?"

"Because your cousin is a very wealthy woman," he replied, seeing no reason to deny the truth. "I will not have any fortune hunters taking advantage of her."

"You honestly believe I would abduct my own cousin?" the viscount shouted. "Are you mad?"

Straightening up from the desk, Nicholas tugged down on his waistcoat. "You are broke. A rich wife would solve all your problems."

The viscount stormed towards him but was stopped by Everett jumping up and placing his hand on his chest. "How dare you!" he exclaimed, pointing at him.

"My job is to protect Penelope from all threats, including family." Nicholas took a step closer to him. "If you wish to see your cousin, then you will abide by my rules." His words were spoken in a tone that brooked no argument.

"I will for now, but I still plan to fight you for guardianship," the viscount threatened.

"I wish you luck." Nicholas smirked.

Lord Mountgarret narrowed his eyes. "You are an arrogant bas…"

"Cousin," Penelope's animated voice came from the doorway. "I thought I heard your voice."

Instantly, Lord Mountgarret's anger melted away, and he turned to face Penelope with a smile on his face. "Yes, his grace has been gracious enough to allow me to call on you."

Penelope's eyes sought him out, and she gave him a look of gratitude. "Thank you, Nicholas."

He would do anything to see her look at him like that again. *Anything.*

"You are welcome. Why don't you go spend time with your cousin in the blue drawing room?"

As he watched them depart from the room, Everett came to stand next to him. "You are allowing Lord Mountgarret, a known fortune hunter, to spend time with your ward?"

"Penelope considers him to be an honorable person."

Everett turned towards him. "Do you?"

"Time will tell," he said frankly. "If he slips up for even a moment, I will ensure that he will never see Penelope again."

"Just for the record, this has nothing to do with your feelings towards Penelope?" his friend asked knowingly.

"Penelope is my ward. Nothing more."

"Ah, you are still in denial."

"Do shut up," he stated.

Everett chuckled. "Is Lord Mountgarret's visit the reason you can't go riding?"

Nicholas was finished with this ridiculous conversation, and he went around his desk. "I have work to do," he declared, sitting down in his chair.

Everett walked over and picked up his top hat. He dusted off the top as he said, "I'm glad that you finally acknowledged that what happened to Alfred was an accident."

"I am beginning to see things more clearly now," he confessed.

The marquess placed his hat on top of his head. "I have a feeling your perspective is changing due to the help of your pretty charge."

Nicholas grunted in response as he shifted his gaze back towards the piles of papers on his desk.

Once Everett reached the door, he turned back around. "It was a good thing you did here today. You made Penelope very happy."

Nicholas watched Everett depart as he realized that at some point Penelope's happiness had come before his own.

12

"I AM SO PLEASED THAT YOU ARE HERE," PENELOPE SAID, leading her cousin into the blue drawing room.

Baldwin grinned. "It was quite a surprise when I received the missive from his grace."

"He is full of surprises," she remarked as she gracefully lowered herself down on the sofa.

Her cousin muttered something under his breath that she couldn't catch. Baldwin sat down next to her, and concern was etched on his face.

"Are you safe here?" he asked, his eyes darting between the four footmen stationed in the room.

"I am."

He leaned closer and whispered, "I have contacted the magistrate. I am contesting the duke's guardianship over you."

"That's not necessary," she protested.

By the frown on his face, it was clear that Baldwin was not convinced. "You are sheltered and inexperienced in the ways…"

"Do not finish that sentence. I am eighteen years old," Penelope warned, cutting him off.

"That proves my point." Her cousin's tone and penetrating

glare caught her off-guard. He had never spoken to her this way before. "Have you considered that the duke may be keeping you a prisoner so he can have you for himself?"

"How dare you make such an outlandish accusation!"

Baldwin jabbed a hand through his hair. "Are you not being kept against your will at Hereford Hall?"

"He is a little zealous with my protection," she paused, when her cousin emitted a disbelieving huff, "but Nicholas…"

"Nicholas?" Baldwin repeated. "I find it odd that you were given leave to call the duke by his given name."

"He is my guardian."

"Surely you agree that he is not a suitable guardian for you," he pressed.

"Why ever not? He was a decorated captain in His Majesty's Royal Navy."

He lowered his voice. "As I mentioned before, there were questionable circumstances surrounding the death of his grace's older brother."

"That's rubbish!" she exclaimed, waving a hand in the air. "It was a horrible accident, nothing more."

"You spoke to the duke about his involvement?"

"Of course I did," she stated, growing defensive. "I consider Nicholas to be an honorable man."

Baldwin's expression grew forlorn. "I am worried about you, Cousin."

Hearing the distress in his tone caused her frustrations to melt away. He was just concerned about her.

"I am well. The duchess has been most gracious, and I have enjoyed my time with her. She reminds me so much of my own mother."

"Your mother was an incredible woman."

"As was yours."

Baldwin sat back in his seat and shifted his gaze towards the footmen. "I won't pursue contesting the duke's guardianship," he hesitated, before adding, "if you promise to come to me if you feel threatened or scared."

"Agreed." She smiled. "Now, can you explain to me why you were about to call the duke a rather offensive name?"

He let out a groan. "You heard that?"

"All of Grosvenor Street heard you," she joked. "Why do you think I interrupted when I did? I believe insulting a duke is a social taboo."

"Trust me, he deserved it."

She laughed. "I have no doubt."

He yanked down on the lapels of his blue riding jacket. "He made an outlandish accusation."

"Let me guess," she started, "he suggested you might want to abscond with me to Gretna Green."

Baldwin gave her a look of disbelief. "How long were you standing there?"

"Just at the end, but Nicholas had told me something similar on a previous occasion," she shared.

His brows furrowed together as he studied her. "How close are you and the duke?"

"We are friends," she replied, glancing over at the footmen.

"Just friends?"

She pursed her lips. "I do not like your insinuation, Cousin."

Putting his hands up, he replied, "I apologize. You two just appear to be closer than what a guardian and his charge should be."

"You're spouting nonsense, and I do not wish to continue this line of questioning," she declared.

"As you wish," he agreed. "Back to our previous conversation; your guardian has agreed to allow me to call on you, assuming they are supervised visits." He tilted his head towards the footmen. "Hence the guards."

"Don't fret. Whenever a gentleman comes to call, the duchess normally accompanies me to greet them." She smirked.

"You should have been here when Lord Tankerville asked me to take a turn around the gardens. I thought Nicholas was going to challenge him to a duel."

"Don't you find that odd?" Baldwin asked. "Normally guardians want their charges to marry quickly."

A piece of her brown hair fell across her face, and she tucked it back behind her ear. "Nicholas and I have agreed that I can pick my own suitor. I plan to marry for love."

Baldwin's countenance grew dim as his gaze shifted towards the floor. "I wish you luck with that."

She reached out and placed her hand on his sleeve. "Did I say something wrong?"

"No," he assured her. "I don't have that same luxury."

"Why ever not?"

He forced a smile. "His grace was correct in the assumption that I need to find a rich wife. If not, I stand to lose everything my family has worked so hard to achieve."

"I happen to be wealthy. I'll give you the money you need," she announced, giving him a triumphant smile.

"No, no, no," he protested. "Absolutely not! I appreciate your kind offer, but I will not accept your money." She opened her mouth to object, but he continued. "Promise me that you will not get involved."

"That's just ridiculous!" she exclaimed. "You are family."

"Cousin, promise me," he said, his voice becoming firm.

Reluctantly, she replied, "I promise."

Baldwin reached out and placed his hand over hers. "I will settle my own matters. You focus on finding a love match."

A loud clearing of a throat came from the doorway, causing her to turn her head to see the duke's imposing figure. He had a scowl on his face. "Time is up, Lord Mountgarret. Unhand my ward and get out."

Her cousin chuckled dryly. "You did not specify I had a time limit with my cousin."

Nicholas stepped further into the room. "Penelope and I need to leave for an appointment."

"May I call on you tomorrow?" Baldwin asked her.

Nicholas answered for her. "You may."

Her cousin's gaze didn't leave hers as he clarified, "I wasn't asking you, your grace. I was asking my cousin."

Penelope rolled her eyes. "Oh, dear. You two are acting like barbarians." She rose and kissed her cousin's cheek. "I look forward to seeing you tomorrow."

She turned towards Nicholas and said, "Allow me to collect my shawl. I'll meet you in the entrance hall."

Nicholas gave her a curt nod before he turned his heated glare back towards her cousin. Good heavens! Was it really so hard for these two to get along?

If only they stopped this silly feud, then they might recognize how similar they were.

Sitting across from Penelope in the coach, Nicholas kept his gaze firmly out the window as he attempted to keep himself distracted from the delightful aroma of vanilla drifting off her person. He was kidding himself. He may not be looking at Penelope, but he had her image etched in his mind. She was wearing a primrose colored gown and a matching bonnet sat in her lap. Long brown curls framed her face, and he had an immense desire to reach out and touch one.

"Thank you for accompanying me to my meeting with Mr. Pratt," she said, drawing his attention.

"You're welcome."

Nicholas started to turn his gaze back towards the window

when she spoke up again. "Your mother wanted me to ask if you plan to attend Lord Misgrove's ball tomorrow evening."

He lifted a brow. "Will you be attending?"

"I will be."

Lowering his brow, he replied, "Then so will I." He saw her eyes light up and added, "After all, you are my ward."

The corners of her lips twitched. "May I ask a favor then?"

"It depends," he stated cautiously.

"Will you not glower so much?"

"I do not glower," he huffed.

She pointed knowingly at his lips. "You do, and you are now."

Nicholas turned his attention back towards the window until he felt her finger tapping on his knee. "May I ask what you are doing?"

"I'm trying to get your attention." Penelope leaned back in her seat with an amused look on her face. "I ask only because I am hoping that gentlemen will approach me to request a dance."

"Not all gentlemen are worthy to dance with you," he pointed out.

The coach lurched to a stop. Nicholas glanced out the window and saw a guarded, gated entrance of a large white warehouse. His driver and the guard spoke for a moment before the gate was pushed to the side, allowing the coach entry.

They rolled slowly along as workers unloaded crates from a merchant ship docked next to the warehouse. Through the window, he heard the sound of men shouting orders. A loud crashing noise came from outside, quickly followed by a string of expletives that reminded him of being on a frigate. He closed the drape, but that did little to keep out the noise.

Nicholas reached under the bench, slid out a metal box, and procured a pistol.

"Do you believe the warehouse is a dangerous place?"

"Anything by the docks is dangerous," he answered as he

tucked it into his waistband. "It's always better to be over-prepared than under. The enemy will not give you an opportunity to arm yourself."

She glanced down at the second weapon in the box. "May I have a pistol as well?"

"Why would you need a pistol?"

"To protect myself."

Nicholas brushed aside her comment as the front wheel dropped in a hole, causing the coach to dip low. He pulled the drape aside before adding, "You are under my protection. You need not fear."

Reaching down, Penelope picked up the pistol before he could stop her. "You won't always be around. It would make sense for me to..." She gasped when he reached over, grabbed her wrist, twisting it to the side and stripped her of the pistol.

He held the pistol up in front of her. "Be serious, Penelope. A pistol is a deadly weapon."

"Will you not teach me?"

Returning the pistol to the metal box, Nicholas chuckled. "You cannot possibly be serious. Ladies are not taught the art of self-defense."

"Good thing I am not a lady," she joked.

Nicholas let his eyes roam over her, from the dark brown hair piled high on top of her head, showing off her elegant neck, to her beautifully-crafted face. Reluctantly, he brought his gaze back up to her deep blue eyes and saw a blush staining her cheeks. He must have been staring longer than he had intended.

"You may not have a title, but you are most assuredly a lady," he responded in a hoarse voice.

Penelope diverted her gaze from him as the coach jerked to a stop. He waited for a footman to open the door before he stepped out and saw Mr. Joseph Pratt and his son waiting near the entrance of the warehouse. He tipped his head in acknowledgement before he turned back around and assisted Penelope out of the carriage.

Now wearing her bonnet, his ward placed her hand into his, but he felt her tense as she glanced nervously around at all the workers who had stopped to watch her exit the carriage. He squeezed her hand in encouragement, hoping his unspoken support would be enough. It was. He saw her chin tilt up, and she exited the coach without any further hesitation. That was his determined Penelope. His Penelope. He liked the sound of that.

Taking her hand, he tucked it into the crook of his elbow. "This is all yours," he said, taking his other hand and waving it over the warehouse and the merchant ships. "You own all of this and more."

Nicholas watched as she scanned the warehouse, the open storage space and the two ships that were docked nearby. To his fascination, she turned and started to acknowledge the dingy workers that were still watching her. Their dirtied faces, mussed hair, and raggedy demeanor, did not seem to intimidate her, and she genuinely smiled at her workers.

Joseph went to approach them, but Nicholas gave him a hard look, indicating he did not want Penelope to be interrupted. As a captain, he knew the importance of meeting his crew and allowing each member to know that they were valued as an individual.

The workers with caps swiped them off their heads as the men started returning her smile. These hardened men found joy in Penelope's smile.

"I am so glad that I came here today," she stated.

His eyes landed on her lips as he asked in disbelief, "How do you do that?"

"Do what?"

"How is it possible that your smile brings joy to everyone around you?"

Her fingers tightened around his arm as she said, "Everyone

could do with a little more kindness in their lives, and a smile is the easiest way to warm someone else's heart."

Nicholas found himself returning her gaze, amazed by the compassion he felt from her.

Mr. Joseph Pratt walked up to them with his arms wide out and a welcoming smile on his face. "Welcome to the Foster Company. Why don't we tour the warehouse and step away from these gawking men?"

He felt Penelope stiffen. "Actually, I would prefer to start the tour outside and finish in the warehouse," she directed in a confident voice.

Joseph's smile dimmed. "As you wish, Miss Foster."

Without delay, Penelope started tugging on Nicholas' arm, directing him towards the ship currently being unloaded. "I thought you might enjoy starting the tour on the ship."

His grin turned into a wide smile as he placed his foot onto the gangway. It felt like home.

❧ 13 ❧

PENELOPE WATCHED THE HAPPINESS RADIATE FROM NICHOLAS AS he explained the various components of the ship. After the tour, he led her to the main deck and started to regale her with stories of his days as a captain. She heard the wistfulness in his tone, causing her heart to mourn for him. He missed being a captain. He missed the sea.

As he started to escort her back towards the gangway, she asked, "Do you ever long to return to the sea?"

"I do," he paused, glancing over at her, "at least, I did."

She gave him a curious look. "What changed?"

Turning his gaze back towards the ship, he appeared reflective. "My priorities changed," he replied.

The gangway swayed under her feet, and she gripped Nicholas' arm tighter to steady herself.

"I am sorry you had to give up your passion to become the duke."

"It was time I came home. Thanks to you, I realized that I had been punishing myself for far too long," Nicholas said, placing his other hand over hers.

She leaned closer to him as the noise of the courtyard intensified. "You are a clever man. I have no doubt you would have figured it out... eventually," she teased.

Glancing over his shoulder at the ship behind them, he remarked, "I am surprised you were not anxious to tour a ship, considering..." His voice stilled as he grimaced.

She understood his hesitancy and appreciated his comment even more. "My parents died during a boating accident but that doesn't make me hate the water. Bad things happen to good people, but it is how we react to those situations that define us."

He smiled over at her. "You are very wise for your age."

"I am, aren't I?" she joked, tilting her chin up.

"And very humble, I see."

Penelope let out an amused laugh as they approached the group of well-dressed men standing in front of the warehouse. Mr. Pratt and his son, Dudley, were conversing with each other, but broke off from them as they neared.

Mr. Pratt gave them a forced smile. "Are you finished with your inspection of the ship?"

"I am," she replied graciously. "Thank you for indulging me and his grace."

Gesturing towards the door, Mr. Pratt said, "Please allow me to give you a tour of the warehouse. I assure you it is more than impressive."

Dudley opened the door for her, and the duke stood aside as she entered. However, Nicholas placed his hand on the small of her back as he followed closely behind. She stepped further into the warehouse and found herself staring in awe. It was a large open facility, with long, narrow windows spanning the length of the walls, and a countless number of well-organized crates and barrels were stacked. Long passageways broke the room into sections.

Penelope turned back towards Joseph and began asking questions, but Dudley was already by her side. He had his arms clasped behind his back as he asked, "Isn't it fascinating? You own all of this merchandise."

"This is all mine?"

He shrugged one shoulder. "The Foster Company acquires these products and then sells them to places all over the world. As I informed you earlier, we pride ourselves on finding the rarest, the most valuable, the most... impossible."

He gestured towards a long passageway. "Shall we?" he asked.

There were so many crates piled high on both sides of them that they barely were able to walk side by side down the narrow aisles.

"Is there anything particular you would like to see?" Dudley glanced over at her. "Perhaps the new shipment of silk we received from India yesterday?"

"I would, very much," she acknowledged.

As Dudley led her towards the far left of the warehouse, he said, "I apologize for my father's insensitive remarks at our last meeting." He gave her a playful smile. "I assure you that my father and I do not see eye-to-eye on everything."

"That's good to hear, Mr. Pratt," she replied, finding herself returning his smile.

"Ah, here we are." Dudley stopped at a crate, and he grabbed a crowbar laying on top of the lid. "I had anticipated your desire to see the finest silk, so I had the workers set this crate aside."

He placed the crowbar under the lid and jerked it open. Grabbing the lid, he laid it down as Penelope took a step closer. Inside the crate was the most beautiful bright blue silk fabric with a gold trim.

She looked over at Dudley for permission. "May I?"

"You don't need to ask permission. Remember, this all belongs to you," he stated as he placed the crowbar back on the ground.

Reaching out, she ran her fingers along the silky material.

The duke stepped closer to her. "This fabric is exquisite," he acknowledged before he turned back to speak to Joseph.

"It is," she murmured, her fingers still sliding along the silk.

Dudley moved to stand on the other side of the crate. "I am glad to hear that. I took the liberty of having some material delivered to Hereford Halls for your enjoyment."

She gasped. "That was most generous of you."

Looking amused, he responded, "Again, I did nothing that is worthy of your praise. This material is yours."

"It seems to me that keeping all of the product is hardly a way to run a business," Penelope joked, dropping the material back into the crate.

Dudley let out a low chuckle. "You are right, Miss Foster." He reached down and picked up the lid. As he placed it back onto the top of the crate, he said in a low voice, "But I thought the blue silk would look lovely on you."

Penelope found her cheeks growing warm with his comment and quickly ducked her chin. She was not accustomed to men saying such flowery words.

Dudley came to stand next to her and offered his arm. "The majority of this imported merchandise will be sold throughout the shops in London, but some of these items are scheduled to be exported," he explained, leading her back down the aisle. "It may surprise you, but within the next few days all of these crates will either be relocated to various businesses or placed onto one of your many merchant ships."

"All these crates?" she asked in disbelief.

He nodded. "Yes. These products will be sold in ports around the world while more items are procured and sent back to replace the inventory. There is a continuous flow of product coming in and out of this warehouse."

Her eyes scanned along all the crates, wondering how that was even possible. "I am impressed," she said.

Dudley sighed in relief. "I am glad. Frankly, my father and I were concerned when Mr. Fulton requested all the company's books for the past five years."

"I had asked Mr. Fulton to familiarize himself with the ledgers so he could explain the company's finances to me," she explained.

"I would be more than willing to tutor you on the various aspects of your company," he assured her.

"Truly?" she asked. "After all, I had assumed you would be busy running the business."

"I will gladly assist you in any way I can."

Penelope started to respond when he placed his hand over hers, causing her immediate discomfort. It wasn't just that he had placed his hand in a familiar fashion, but it was the fact that it wasn't Nicholas.

Immediately, she slipped her hand out from under his. "Thank you, but I believe it would be best for Mr. Fulton to tutor me."

Dudley wore an apologetic smile on his face. "I apologize for my boldness. Is there an understanding between you and his grace?"

"No understanding," she replied quickly. "He is merely my guardian."

Glancing behind them at the duke and his father, Dudley turned his gaze back towards her and lowered his voice. "Surely you jest?"

"Why do you say such a thing?" she asked.

With a furrowed brow, he explained, "His grace does not look at you like a man would look at his charge, but rather the way a man would look at his betrothed."

She frowned. "That's rubbish. The duke considers me a step above a nuisance."

Dudley watched her as if he was gauging her sincerity. "Perhaps I'm wrong." He pointed towards a door in the back of the warehouse. "If you will follow me to the office, I would like to introduce you to all the men on the board of your company."

Penelope glanced over her shoulder to watch the duke. Did she dare believe that he held her in some regard? No, that was impossible. Dudley must be mistaken.

She had no doubt that his grace was counting down the days until she was no longer his burden.

Nicholas sat alone in his study, the silence broken only by the sounds of the crackling fire in the hearth. After dinner, his mother and Penelope had moved to the drawing room to play games, but he was not in the mood to engage in light speech. It was getting harder not to pull Penelope into his arms and confess his feelings.

He grunted, loudly. What a horrible guardian he was turning out to be. He was supposed to protect his charge, not fall in love with her.

His mother's smoothing voice came from the doorway. "I was preparing to retire for the evening, but I saw the light on." She walked further into the room. "Are you feeling all right, dear?"

"Nothing to concern yourself about, Mother," he replied in a sharper tone than he intended.

Mildred approached and sat down next to him, not deterred by his rude tongue. "I was pleased when Penelope informed me that you will be attending Lord Misgrove's ball with us tomorrow evening."

He gave her a forced smile. "It will be my pleasure."

"Will it now?" she asked deliberately.

"Penelope is my charge, and I need to ensure her protection," he asserted. "I can hardly send along ten footmen to guard her on the dance floor."

His mother angled herself towards him. "I see," she murmured. "So, it has nothing to do with your attraction towards her?"

"I am not attracted to Penelope," he lied, the words tasting bitter in his mouth. He rose and walked over to the drink tray. "She is my ward."

"It is not illegal to marry your ward. In fact, it's a lot more common than you realize."

Taking off the decanter lid, Nicholas stiffened at her words. "Regardless, I do not intend to marry."

"May I ask why?"

He poured himself a brandy, replacing the lid before answering. "Marriage is for fools, and I am no fool."

The duchess smiled at him. "At least you have a reason," she paused, "albeit, a weak one."

He tossed back his drink and placed the glass onto the drink cart. "The institution of marriage is designed to repress both individuals, forcing them to seek out happiness from outside their bonds of matrimony."

His mother leaned back against the sofa as she wore a mask of indifference, making it impossible to gauge her reaction to his blunt words. Her words started out slow. "You have every right to be cynical based on your own experience, but not every marriage is like your father's and mine. Our parents arranged our marriage when we were very young, and we both accepted our fates."

He spun to face her, outraged. "Father was a monster. He beat us. He beat you!"

"John faced incredible pressure as the second son of a duke. He was attempting to live up to his family's unrealistic expectations...."

"You will not defend him!" he shouted, advancing towards

her. He stopped next to the sofa. "I lived in fear growing up, and after Alfred died…" His words hitched with emotions. "I knew I had to leave and never look back."

His mother's eyes filled with compassion. "I know. Your father said incredibly cruel things to you, but he didn't believe you were responsible for Alfred's death."

"No?" he scoffed. "He could have fooled me."

"We all were grieving Alfred's death in different ways. One is never prepared to lose a son in such a horrific accident."

He pressed his lips together to prevent his emotions from raging out of control. "I am sorry…"

His mother rose and embraced him before he even finished his words. "You have nothing to apologize for, son. You were injured as well from the fall, and yet, you rushed back to find help. Your actions were nothing but heroic."

Nicholas shook his head, not daring to believe her words. How could she forgive him so easily? "It was my fault for suggesting that we should explore the ruins."

The duchess leaned back and moved her hand to cup his right cheek. "You have always carried a mantle of responsibility for others on your shoulders. Perhaps that's why you were such a remarkable captain. But it was also why you endured the brunt of your father's heavy hand."

"No, Father beat all of us."

A soft smile came to his mother's face. "True, but at eight, do you recall stepping in front of me and demanding that he strike you and not me?"

The faintest recollection came to his mind, but it didn't change anything. Any boy would try to protect his mother.

She spoke up again. "Alfred wasn't as physically strong as you. He got along just fine, but he had a weak heart. Which is why you would always step in and fight his battles as well." A lone tear dropped down onto his mother's cheek. "You two boys were my greatest joy, and it broke my heart when I lost both of you that day."

"You didn't lose me, Mother," he whispered, "I just chose a different path for myself. I had to leave."

Her eyes filled with tears. "I know, but it still broke my heart."

"I am sorry I left you with Father," he whimpered, the years of regret finally catching up to him.

"Don't be. After you left, John packed his trunks and started living openly with his mistress. We hardly spoke to each other all the years you were at sea." She stepped back and swiped at her cheeks. "I found out about his death when his solicitor came to offer his condolences."

The fire crackled in the hearth as he said, "You didn't deserve father's ill-treatment."

"I did not, but I chose to go along with the marriage," she admitted. "I could have fought the betrothal agreement. I could have run away and had a simpler life. However, I made a choice," she hesitated, her voice hitching, "and that choice gave me you and Alfred. I would do it again to be your mother."

Nicholas ducked his head in embarrassment for his own poor treatment of his mother. He had neglected her all these years.

She placed her hand on his sleeve. "You have given so much of yourself over these years and it is time that you made a choice." She waited till he raised his gaze to hers. "Do you want Penelope as your wife?"

He winced. "She wants a love match."

"Is that a problem?" his mother asked.

"I care for her... immensely, but I hardly know her," he pressed.

"That is poppy-cock, and you know it," she countered, removing her hand from his sleeve.

He breathed a loud, heartfelt sigh. "Even if by some miraculous chance that Penelope accepts my suit, I am not worthy of her."

"You are a duke, a war-hero…" his mother started listing off.

Nicholas spoke over her. "I am not referring to titles or positions that I have held, but the whole essence of my being. Penelope is beautiful, clever, witty, and obnoxiously cheerful. She speaks in a manner that somehow penetrates my heart, breaking through all my doubts and fears."

He turned his gaze back towards the fire in the hearth, attempting to ignore the growing smile on his mother's face. What would he do if Penelope chose another? He already knew the answer. She would take his heart with her.

"You need to tell her, and quickly," his mother urged softly.

"What if she doesn't return my feelings?" he asked, nervously meeting her gaze.

Taking a few steps closer, his mother patted his cheek. "I never said it would be easy, but Penelope is a girl worth risking everything for. I believe she is your love match."

"I will tell her of my feelings tomorrow," he reluctantly agreed.

"Good. Now, I am off to bed," his mother said as she turned to leave. Once she reached the door, she spun back around. "Good night, dear."

"Good night," he murmured.

How could he possibly sleep now?

❧ 14 ❧

NICHOLAS' BLASTED DUTIES KEPT HIM BUSY ALL DAY LONG. Being a duke certainly wasn't all about leisure! Between meetings, reviewing the ledgers, and going to the House of Lords for a vote in the evening, he had not had one moment alone with Penelope all day. He missed her smile. Her infectious personality. He just missed her.

He adjusted his cravat as he waited at the bottom of the stairs. The ladies should be down any minute, and they would all depart for Lord Misgrove's ball.

Nicholas heard Penelope's voice before he saw her. He glanced up the stairs, and he found himself rendered speechless by her beauty. She was wearing a white, high-waisted ball gown that hugged her curves in a glorious fashion. Her hair was styled high upon her head and curls ran down the length of her back.

He continued to watch her as she gracefully walked down the stairs and stopped in front of him. She held out the skirt for his inspection. "What do you think?"

Unable to stop himself, he slipped his arm around her waist and whispered in her ear, "You will be the most beautiful woman in the room." He felt Penelope shudder as he spoke, and it filled him with hope. Perhaps she would accept his suit.

"Good heavens. Do not accost the dear girl, Nicholas," his mother stated from the top of the stairs.

Reluctantly, he removed his arm from around her waist and stepped back. "I was merely commenting on how beautiful she looks this evening," he said, giving Penelope a wink.

Penelope blushed adorably as she turned her gaze towards Mildred. "Your mother was kind enough to let me borrow a necklace this evening," she informed him, fingering the large diamond necklace.

"That was most kind of her," Nicholas acknowledged. "Shall we?" He extended his arms towards the ladies and started leading them towards the coach.

Despite Lord Misgrove's townhouse being only a few blocks away, it still took a considerable amount of time to arrive at the main entrance because of the long line of carriages waiting to be unloaded. "This looks like a crush," his mother remarked in an excited tone.

"How grand," Penelope murmured as she kept her gaze out the window.

His mother tapped Penelope's knee with the fan in her hand. "Do you remember all the instructions I gave to you earlier?"

She gave the duchess her full attention. "Yes, your grace. I won't dance with any gentleman more than once, I will insist that my dance partner will return me to you or the duke, and I won't drink more than one flute of champagne."

"You only gave me three rules," his mother said in a jovial tone. "What about the other hundred that I discussed with you?"

Penelope clasped her hands in her lap. "Do you truly wish for me to repeat all of them?"

"There's no need," Nicholas declared. "I won't be leaving your side the entire evening."

Penelope rewarded him with a bright smile. "I won't

complain. I was taught social etiquette at the finishing school, but your mother found it lacking. She has inundated me with thousands of society's rules, and I daresay I could never remember them all."

Nicholas let out an exaggerated sigh. "Do not let my mother fill your head with useless information."

"It's not useless," the duchess replied, flipping her fan open. "Even the way she holds her fan is crucial to her success."

"I can teach her," he said.

"You?" His mother snapped the fan shut.

"Allow me." Nicholas held his hand out, and she extended the fan towards him. He flipped it open and fanned his face. "This means I am overly warm." He snapped the fan and tapped Penelope on the shoulder. "This action means I am challenging your fan to a duel."

Penelope laughed. "How can two fans duel?"

The coach rolled to a stop, and the door was opened. "I guess we will never know now," he joked as he handed the fan back to his mother.

Nicholas stepped out and turned to assist the ladies. He started escorting them inside, and he noticed that Penelope kept glancing his way. Keeping his head straight, he asked, "Is everything all right?"

She puckered her brow. "You seem different tonight."

"Is that a good thing or a bad thing?" he questioned.

He expected her to reply it was a good thing, so he was surprised when she said, "Neither. I find all of your moods to be *tolerable*."

Nicholas chuckled under his breath. "Tolerable?"

"If you are looking for flattery from me, then you will be sorely disappointed," she asserted with a stoic face, although, the corners of her lips twitched with amusement.

As they walked further into the rectangular ballroom, the

crowds intensified, and they could barely see the maroon-papered walls with the gold-leafed accents. Large chandeliers hung low and hundreds of lighted candles made the room obnoxiously warm.

Nicholas led them towards the back of the ballroom where two French doors were open, bringing in the cool night air and offering them a welcome relief.

Everett came up from behind him. "I thought I heard you being announced!" he shouted to be heard over the noise in the ballroom.

His mother and Penelope dropped their hands and turned towards Everett.

"Your grace," Lord Northampton said respectfully to the duchess. Then he turned and acknowledged Penelope. "Miss Foster, you are looking breathtaking this evening."

Penelope curtsied. "Thank you, Lord Northampton."

Nicholas did not like the way that Everett was looking at his ward, so he stepped closer to her. "Did you come alone this evening?"

Everett gave him a smug smile. "I did, in fact." He asked his next question to Penelope. "Will you save me a dance?"

She tilted her head in acknowledgement. "I would be honored."

"Excellent," Everett stated. "I will be back later to collect you. I plan to avoid the scheming mothers by staying in the card room." He bowed. "If you will excuse me."

The orchestra had finished warming up and was preparing to start playing for the first dance set. As much as Nicholas wanted to ask Penelope to dance the first set, he would much rather ask her to dance the waltz.

He was about to ask Penelope if she would like something to drink when her cousin, Lord Mountgarret, walked up to her with a smile on his face. "What a pleasant surprise. I had no idea you were attending the ball this evening." He bowed as he acknowledged the duchess politely, but scowled at him while saying, "Your grace."

Nicholas narrowed his eyes at Lord Mountgarret. "Last I heard you were still at the House of Lords attempting to justify the need for social reform."

"That sounds exciting," Penelope's animated voice exclaimed as her eyes darted between them.

Baldwin shifted his gaze towards his cousin. "Would you like to dance the first set?"

"I would be honored, assuming his grace has no objections," she said in a tone that implied he would have no objections.

He tipped his head graciously. "By all means, go enjoy yourselves, but please return Miss Foster back to me at the end of the set."

"I have every intention to," Baldwin remarked dryly. "After all, Penelope does not belong to me. Or anyone, for that matter."

Nicholas never had such a desire to flog a person as he did with Lord Mountgarret. He managed to fake a smile for his ward's sake. "You are correct."

As he watched Penelope disappear into the crowd with Baldwin, Nicholas ground his teeth.

His mother opened her fan and started fanning her face. "Lord Mountgarret seems like a fine young man."

Rather than contradict his mother, Nicholas decided his time would be better spent keeping a close eye on his ward.

Penelope felt like she was in a dream. For years, a dance master had instructed her on the various styles of dances, but she had never had a gentleman as a partner. She had always been partnered with one of the girls at the school.

After each dance, she barely had a moment to catch her breath before another gentleman came up to collect her for the next dance. It was exhilarating.

She had just finished dancing the quadrille with Lord Ryder when he extended his arm towards her and started leading her back to her guardian.

"You are an excellent dance partner, Miss Foster," he said with a flirtatious smile. "Perhaps I could call on you tomorrow, and we could go for a carriage ride through Hyde Park?"

Penelope diverted her gaze from the attractive lord. Going on a ride did sound fun, but she would prefer to go on a ride with Nicholas. Not Lord Ryder. Not any other gentleman.

"I'm afraid the duchess and I will not be taking callers tomorrow," she lied. "Another time, perhaps?"

Not deterred by her rejection, Lord Ryder's eyes roamed over her face, and she could see desire in his eyes. "I will call the following day and hope you will be home to receive me."

She knew the moment that Lord Ryder caught sight of the Duke of Blackbourne, because she felt him go rigid.

"Lord Ryder," Nicholas said sternly as they approached. His eyes lowered to her hand on the Lord's arm, and he frowned.

Lord Ryder dropped his arm to his side and stepped away from her. He bowed. "Your grace," he started, "thank you for allowing me the privilege of dancing with your ward."

Nicholas' frown deepened as the young man straightened and turned towards Penelope. Lord Ryder reached for her hand but stopped when the duke grunted his disapproval. Instead, he spoke quickly. "I will call on you shortly." Then, he disappeared into the crowd.

Penelope placed her hand on her hip and turned to face Nicholas. "That was uncalled for. You can't scare off every potential suitor."

She swore she saw a flash of panic enter the duke's eyes, but it disappeared just as quickly, making her think she just imagined it.

"Are you saying you might entertain an offer from Lord Ryder?"

Penelope could have lied, could have seen if Nicholas would become jealous, but instead she decided to tell the truth. She shook her head. "No. I am not interested in Lord Ryder."

"Good," he proclaimed.

It was announced that the next dance would be the waltz. She sighed a breath of relief. At last, she would be able to sit down for one dance. "Would you mind if we sat..." Her words were stopped when the duke placed his hand on her elbow and started escorting her towards the dance floor. "What are you doing?"

He looked amused by her question. "We are dancing the waltz."

"I can't. In order to dance the waltz, I need permission from the patroness of the dance."

"I already obtained it," he informed her as they stepped out onto the chalked dance floor. He went to stand in front of her. "Are you ready to dance with me?"

A thrill coursed through her body as she nodded her answer. Penelope couldn't seem to find the adequate words to express how desperately she wanted to dance with him. Time seemed to slow as he gently slipped his arm around her waist, drawing her closer. She managed to remember to place one gloved hand onto his shoulder, curling the other in his palm.

As he started guiding her to the music, Penelope felt everything else fading away as she focused on Nicholas. He was watching her with such intensity, and dare she believe, longing, that she found herself transfixed. Never had a man looked at her like that before. It was intoxicating.

Nicholas raised their hands above their heads and now their faces were only inches apart. No wonder this dance was so scandalous. She watched as his eyes dropped to her lips, and her heart lurched in her chest. Could the duke actually want to kiss her?

Their hands came down, and she missed the nearness of him. Why would Nicholas ever be interested in someone like her? She was young, sheltered, and a burden to him. He cleared his throat, and she was mortified to realize that she had been staring at his lips.

Her cheeks grew increasingly warm as he commented, "You dance exceptionally well, Penelope."

"Thank you," she murmured, still refusing to meet his gaze.

When their hands went up, the duke started speaking with profound hesitancy in his voice, something that she had never heard before. "I... uh... have been meaning to speak to you about something important."

Penelope brought her gaze back up. "Is that so?"

His hand tightened around her waist, and he brought her even closer to him. "You are a remarkable young woman, and I have enjoyed our time together. So much, in fact, that I..." His voice trailed off, and she was surprised to see the duke appeared nervous.

Taking pity on him, she remarked, "I have enjoyed our time together as well."

"Good," he murmured with a bob of his head. "That's good to know, especially since I was hard on you at the beginning."

Penelope relaxed in his arms, knowing that she had dreamed of this moment. And now, with him so close, she felt almost breathless. It was where she belonged.

"I hardly blame you," she said, finally finding her voice. "You inherited a rambunctious ward when you became the Duke of Blackbourne."

His eyes intensified. Darkened. "I have now come to realize how blessed I was to become your guardian."

"Truly?" she asked, vaguely acknowledging the music stopping in the background.

Nicholas stopped on the dance floor and reached for her other hand. "Penelope, dear," he began, "I know we started off poorly, but...I... um... have grown to..." He stopped speaking as his eyes darted around the room. "I suggest we go somewhere more private for the remainder of this conversation."

Penelope turned her gaze and saw that all eyes were on them. At some point all the other dancers had exited, but they had remained. Women had fans up to their faces, and they were whispering back and forth to each other. About her. She had never been a public spectacle before, and she found that she did not like it.

Not waiting for Nicholas' escort, she walked swiftly through the crowd, ignoring their blatant stares, and didn't stop until she approached the duchess.

"Are you all right, my dear?" Mildred asked in concern.

She nodded, but her attention was fixated on the French doors leading outside. "I just need a moment alone on the veranda."

"Would you like me to accompany you?"

Penelope shook her head. She wanted to be alone to process what Nicholas had been attempting to tell her. "That's not necessary. I will remain close."

The duchess stepped aside as she said, "As you wish."

Walking outside, Penelope welcomed the cool night air as she wrapped her arms around her waist. She saw women still watching her from the ballroom, judging her. Mocking her.

"Are you all right, Miss Foster?" A male's voice came from the shadows, causing her to jump in surprise.

She relaxed when she recognized Mr. Dudley Pratt stepping out of the darkness of the estate. "You scared me," she replied, bringing her hand up to her chest.

"That was not my intent," he said, "but I wanted to come and see if you were all right."

"You must have seen his grace and me dancing," she murmured, wincing.

He nodded, reluctantly. "I did. Ignore those catty women. We both know that you are not the duke's mistress."

Mistress. Penelope dropped her head as she stepped away from the light of the ballroom. The duchess had warned her that the slightest infraction could ruin her reputation amongst the ton.

Dudley leaned his shoulder against the stone wall. "Would you like me to escort you back to Hereford Hall?"

"No. That would not be a good idea," she stated, glancing over her shoulder at the ballroom. "I better return to her grace before the duke realizes I am gone."

"Wait, before you go," he proclaimed, pushing off the wall. "Come away with me. Marry me, and we could run your company as a partnership."

Penelope was shocked by his offer, but she managed to recover quickly. "I am flattered but…"

Dudley took a step closer to her while he continued to plead his case. "I won't give you limitations or orders as the duke would. You would be free to do as you please."

Penelope had no desire to inform Dudley that she recognized the rules the duke implemented were designed to keep her safe, not restrict her. She gave him a tentative smile. "I thank you for your offer, but I am happy where I am."

"I understand, but I had to at least make my intentions known. I just hope this won't affect our business association," he remarked, returning her smile.

"Of course not, Mr. Pratt," she replied.

With a parting glance at Dudley, she turned to go back inside. Then everything went black.

❧ 15 ☙

NICHOLAS ATTEMPTED TO REMAIN CORDIAL AS YOUNG WOMEN, and their mothers, kept blocking his path, fluttering their eyelashes. He didn't have time for this. He had seen the hurt flash across Penelope's face as she rushed off the dance floor, practically running from him.

He had been so engrossed with Penelope that he had failed to acknowledge the music had stopped. What had happened to him? He could command the crew of a warship, but he got distracted gazing into his ward's eyes.

Another young woman smiled coyly at him as she dipped into a low curtsy, showing off her ample bosom. "Your grace."

He averted his eyes, tired of these useless interruptions. He only wanted to see Penelope again, to ensure she was all right. How he wished that it was proper for him to bring a pistol to a social gathering. One shot fired in the air would cause these scheming women to depart from his presence.

"Ladies," he growled, causing the women's eyes to widen. "I demand that you clear a path for me."

A few of the women hesitated, but he proceeded to start walking anyway. Within a few moments, a path was created for him, lined with gawking patrons, as he headed straight towards his mother.

The duchess frowned as she held a flute of champagne in her hand. "Would you kindly explain why the room parted like the Red Sea?"

"It matters not," he stated. "Where is Penelope?"

"She requested a moment alone," she answered, waving her hand towards the French doors.

He hesitated, before asking, "Do you think she would mind if I intruded?"

"I doubt it."

Nicholas walked out of the French doors, and his eyes scanned the veranda. "Penelope?" he called out, his voice rising. He walked swiftly down the few steps and onto the path of the well-maintained garden. Still he saw no trace of his ward. "Penelope!" he shouted, causing birds to take flight from the trees. Where was she? She must have slipped back inside without anyone realizing.

He walked swiftly back to his mother and didn't stop until he whispered in her ear, "I can't find Penelope. We need to search for her, discreetly."

The duchess' face grew expressionless. "Go get Everett. The more eyes looking for Penelope, the better."

"I agree."

Nicholas walked as fast as he could through the hordes of guests until he arrived at the game room. The room held ten small round tables where gentlemen were sitting, smoking cigars and drinking brandy. He spotted Everett across the room. Before he even moved from the doorway, his friend looked up and saw him. The panic on his face must have been evident, because Everett pushed back his chair and headed straight for him.

"Whatever is the matter?" Everett asked.

"Penelope is missing." Nicholas didn't say another word as he started towards an empty hall off the ballroom. When Everett matched his stride, he explained, "Penelope stepped outside, and we don't know where she is."

Frowning, his friend asked, "Where were you?"

"I was…" His words were cut off when Lord Mountgarret shoved him against the wall, reared back his arm, and punched him in the jaw.

The viscount may have gotten one lucky punch in, but that was all he was going to get. Nicholas took his fist and pummeled it into Baldwin's stomach, causing him to bend over at the waist, gasping for breath. His left hand held the lapels of the viscount's jacket, and he pulled his other arm back to strike again, but he stopped. As much as he disliked this man, he was important to Penelope. Instead, he shoved him back.

Baldwin glared at Nicholas as he straightened. "You ruined Penelope!"

"Ruined?" he asked in confusion. "How exactly did I ruin her?"

Adjusting his wrinkled waistcoat, Lord Mountgarret replied, "By making her a public spectacle after the waltz. I heard women calling her your 'mistress'."

Mistress. His heart shattered for Penelope. No wonder why she wanted to be alone. "I did no such thing," he declared. "I was attempting to find the right moment to offer for her."

The viscount scoffed. "I knew it. That was your plan all along. To have her for yourself." He started slow clapping. "Well done, you egotistical blackguard."

Nicholas clenched his fists at his side, debating about taking another swing at the man. "What did you do with Penelope?"

Baldwin stopped clapping. "What do you mean? Did you lose my cousin?" He let out a dry chuckle. "This night keeps getting better and better."

Taking a commanding step closer to Baldwin, he grabbed his white shirt and yanked him closer. "If I find that you had anything to do with her disappearance, then I will ruin you."

The viscount shoved him back. "You never learn, do you? I only want my cousin to be happy."

With an annoyed expression on his face, Everett was leaning his back against the wall when he interjected, "If you two are finished fighting, I propose we start looking for Penelope."

Nicholas wanted nothing to do with Lord Mountgarret, but he needed his help to search for Penelope. Nothing else mattered right now. He cleared his throat as he spoke to Baldwin. "Your cousin was last seen on the veranda, but my mother never saw her come inside. I could use your help to find her."

"I will help you, but only for Penelope," he said, voicing his disapproval. "I still find you to be extraordinarily irksome."

"Thank you," Nicholas replied, ignoring the insult. It didn't matter if the viscount hated him. He only cared about finding Penelope.

Everett pushed back off the wall. "It certainly took a ridiculously long time for you two to come to a consensus. Can we please get back to the matter at hand?"

Nicholas took command of the situation. "Everett, go to the front and speak to the servants. Ask if anyone saw Penelope leaving." His friend nodded and disappeared without further direction. He turned towards Baldwin. "Help me walk around the crush. Perhaps Penelope came in undetected."

"For what purpose?" the viscount asked as they started walking towards the ballroom.

Nicholas spared him a glance. "I can't think of one reason."

They split up and searched the various alcoves of the ballroom and looked at everyone standing around. He blatantly ignored the young women that vied for his attention, and a few mothers voiced their haughty outrage at his un-gentlemanly behavior.

Once they arrived back at the French doors, Everett ran up to them with a panicked expression. "At first, no one admitted to seeing anything, but then I offered £5," he informed them as he caught his breath. "An unconscious woman matching Penelope's description was placed into a carriage a short while ago."

"What?!" Nicholas roared, ignoring the disapproving glances from the other patrons.

Grabbing his arm, Everett led him outside and onto the veranda. "When I pressed the footmen for additional information, they confessed that a guest had approached them and informed them that his sister had gotten intoxicated. He paid them each one pound to help him leave undetected."

Baldwin's voice grew low, threatening. "Can they identify the man?"

Everett nodded. "The driver called him Mr. Pratt."

"I am going after them," Nicholas declared as he went to take his first step.

Stepping in front of him to block his exit, Everett's voice was calm and steady. "We must approach this logically. If I were Mr. Pratt, where would I have taken her?"

"Gretna Green," Baldwin answered. "Why else would he have abducted her if he didn't intend to marry her?"

"Of course, you would know the answer," Nicholas replied dryly.

Baldwin huffed. "Why did I agree to help you again?"

"Lord Misgrove is a family friend," Everett informed them. "I am going to borrow three horses and hopefully the dueling pistols that he keeps in his office. I will meet you out front." He turned quickly on his heel and headed inside the ballroom.

Nicholas shouted at his friend's retreating figure, "We only need two horses!"

"Three," Baldwin corrected. "You must be bloody off your cracker if you think I'm not going with you to save my cousin."

"Fine, but this doesn't mean I like you."

"I feel the same way."

They were nearing the main door when Baldwin pointed out, "I find it ironic that you accused me of having nefarious intentions with my cousin, but you failed to recognize Mr. Pratt as a threat."

Nicholas pursed his lips together. "It would be best if we rescued Penelope in silence."

"Agreed."

Penelope's head hurt. It felt like it was between a vice that was slowly tightening. She moaned as she brought her hand up to her forehead. What had happened? Why did she feel so awful?

She recognized the rhythmic sounds of horse hooves hitting the ground, and she felt herself being rocked side to side. Either this was a realistic dream, or she was in a fast-moving coach.

"Good, you are finally awake," a familiar male's voice declared. "It's been hours, and I was worried that I'd hit you harder than I intended."

That voice. Now she remembered. She had been speaking to Mr. Dudley Pratt and had left to go back into the ball. Penelope opened her eyes slowly, and she saw him sitting on the opposite bench. "You are fired, Mr. Pratt," she said sarcastically.

Dudley chuckled. "You are a delight, Penelope."

Lowering her hand from her forehead, she stated, "I never gave you leave to use my given name."

"It won't matter soon enough."

She glanced over at the closed curtain and saw that it was still dark outside. "For what purpose did you abduct me?"

Stretching out his legs, he replied, "To marry you, of course."

"I will never marry you," she responded firmly.

Dudley wore a look of amusement. "You don't have a choice."

Penelope reached up to the back of her head and felt her hair matted with dry blood. "The Duke of Blackbourne is my guardian, and he will never grant permission for us to be wed."

"Scotland has different rules, and no consent is needed," he pointed out. "I have already sent two riders ahead to find a blacksmith that would be willing to overlook your reluctance."

"His grace will come after me," she replied confidently.

Dudley put his hands up over his head, completely unperturbed by her remark. "I anticipate that will be the case, but he will be too late." He smirked. "I let it slip that the duke was looking for a wife, and that he intended to be married by the end of the Season. It might have taken him an hour or so before he even noticed you were missing."

The sleeve of her white gown had slipped off her shoulder and she quickly adjusted it, although, not before she saw Mr. Pratt's eyes lewdly roam over her body. She shuddered. "Why?" she asked. "Why would you go to such extremes to abduct me to be your wife?"

"Well, you are a beautiful woman, Penelope," he said smoothly. "Any man would be lucky to have you as a wife."

She rolled her eyes. "Spare me the flattery, Mr. Pratt."

"You are also exceedingly wealthy, and you have something I want."

"A personality?" she quipped.

Not appearing amused, he replied, "You will find I am a reasonable man, but if you push me too far, then I will punish you for your insolence."

She tilted her chin. "Do you expect me to just sit back and accept my fate?"

"If you are wise, yes."

"Then you don't know me," she asserted. "I will never stop fighting you. I will always try to escape."

In a swift powerful move, Dudley raised his hand and slapped her. "I would be careful of your place. After all, once we are married, your usefulness will be over."

Her cheek throbbed. But she refused to raise her hand to her face and admit she was in pain.

He leaned forward in his seat and grabbed her chin, forcing her to look at him. "This was not my original plan. I had intended to woo you, and then offer for you. However, seeing you dance with the duke at the ball forced me to accelerate my plan."

She maintained his gaze, refusing to cower. Nicholas would come for her, and Dudley would get his comeuppance. Until then, she just had to stay alive. "Why?"

"Because, my dear," he replied, "it was painfully obvious to everyone in the room that you two were in love."

Penelope cringed at Dudley's words. Was her love for Nicholas so obvious to others? Regardless, he did not love her. She was sure of that. "Then why did I hear women whispering that I was his mistress?" she asked, not believing his explanation.

He dropped her chin and leaned back. "The ton is made up of miserable, fickle people. The women aspire to climb the social ladder, and the men just hope to find a woman with a large enough dowry. No one marries for love. But you," he paused, pointing at her, "found love, and that makes people very uncomfortable."

"You are wrong. The duke does not love me," she murmured.

Dudley shrugged. "Either way, it matters not. We will be married soon enough."

Bringing her hand up, she rubbed her tender cheek. "You were already running my company, and I have no doubt that you were paying yourself handsomely," she stated in an annoyed tone. "Why do you need to marry me?"

"That is a ticklish question," he remarked. "After your father died, a lot of the investors lost confidence in our leadership, and we had to doctor our ledgers to show a profitable quarter. However, it was a horrific quarter. We lost a lot of money." He shifted in his seat and adjusted his black jacket. "We found a way to recoup our losses, but it wasn't legal."

"What a stalwart employee you turned out to be," she admonished in a dry tone.

Dudley slapped her again, harder than before, causing her head to hit the side of the carriage. "Do not interrupt me again," he warned in a cold tone. "We found importing slaves to the British colony on the isle of Mauritius to be quite profitable."

Holding her hand up to the side of her head, she felt the blood trickling down her cheek. "Importing slaves is illegal."

Adjusting his cuff links, he stated, "Parliament did pass the Slave Trade Act in 1807 making it illegal for Britons to participate in the trade of enslaved Africans. However, besides creating the anti-slavery squadrons using old, semi-derelict naval vessels, which are unfit for coastal conditions, Britain continues to ignore their own laws about the slave trade. Financing the importing of slaves is extremely profitable for us, Britain, and other countries."

"Regardless, what you are doing is immoral."

"It is what made you wealthier than you could ever imagine," Dudley gave her a cocky smile, "as well as lining my family's pockets."

Penelope studied him, not understanding the cruelty he exhibited. "Why would you enslave people for profit? How much money do you need?"

"I could never have enough money," he said frankly.

"When Nicholas rescues me," Penelope paused, her voice becoming adamant, "because he will rescue me, I promise you will pay for what you have done, both to those slaves and my father's company."

Dudley lowered his gaze towards her rounded neckline, not bothering to hide his desire. "It will be fun to break your willful streak, my dear." He brought his gaze up. "And if I can't, then I will kill you and call it an accident."

Unexpectedly, the carriage jerked to the side, and she placed her hands up on the walls to steady herself. She could hear shouting outside as the carriage rocked back and forth. Dudley grabbed the curtain and peered outside. He let out an expletive, tossing the curtain aside and opening the window.

Dudley reached down and pulled out a metal box from under the bench. He opened it up and produced a pistol. "It looks like your duke will die tonight," he announced, while taking aim out the window.

"No!" Penelope shouted, reaching for the pistol and shoving it up in the air. As they wrestled for the weapon, the coach started slowing down, but she knew what was at risk if she lost this battle. Tightening her hold, she refused to give up.

Dudley took his elbow and slammed it into her face, but still she refused to yield. A loud shot erupted in the coach, and she felt an explosion of pain radiate in her right arm.

She had been shot.

🦋 16 🦋

NICHOLAS URGED HIS HORSE FASTER AS HE SAW THE SPEEDING coach up ahead. He needed to stop that coach and save Penelope. He didn't even want to think about what was at stake if he failed.

A shout rang out from the front of the coach. "Highwaymen!" They had been spotted.

Nicholas grabbed the pistol from the waistband of his trousers and held it in his right hand. A highwayman would have been preferable to him, he thought. He would do whatever it took to get Penelope back into his arms.

He jerked his head towards the driver's side of the coach, alerting Everett and Baldwin of his intentions, then broke off from them. After he passed the back of the coach, the driver veered the coach towards him, hoping to run him off the road. It was a comical attempt. As a captain of a frigate, he had stared the enemy in the eye as cannons were aimed at him, and he had not flinched. The driver of a coach would not be able to stop him.

Raising his pistol, Nicholas kept his arm steady as he aimed it at the driver and ordered, "Stop this coach!" He was not bluffing, and the driver's expression grew fearful.

The driver pulled back on the reins, and the coach began to slow. Then a shot rang out. A shot from inside the carriage.

The moment the coach came to a skidding halt, Nicholas dismounted and wrenched open the door. He saw a bloodied, wide-eyed Penelope, staring back at him, and he felt raw rage grow inside of him. She had been hurt.

"Are you all right?" he asked while he kept his pistol pointed at Mr. Pratt.

She nodded, but he could see the tears forming in her eyes.

Tucking his pistol into the waistband of his trousers, Nicholas reached in, grabbed Mr. Pratt's shirt, and tossed him out of the coach. While the man attempted to stand up, Nicholas grabbed his shirt again, yanked him up, and punched him in the right eye. Then he did it again. And again.

Penelope's panicked voice came from behind him. "Nicholas, *stop*! You are going to kill him!"

His fist reared back again, but he hesitated, realizing that Penelope was witnessing him beating this man to a bloody pulp. He shoved Mr. Pratt to the ground and turned towards his ward.

Her hair was disheveled, her white dress was soiled, and she had blood on her face. But to him, she never looked more beautiful. "Penelope…" His voice hitched with emotion. He was so relieved that she was here. Alive.

Her lower lip trembled as she watched him. She was attempting to be strong. Why? In two strides, he had her wrapped up in his arms. Right where she belonged. His poor, brave Penelope.

Nicholas leaned back only slightly and asked, "Where are you injured?"

"The bullet grazed my arm," she replied, looking down at her right arm.

Nicholas saw the red, blotching skin on her arm, feeling relief that the bullet had only grazed her. He pointed to the dry blood that stained the length of her left cheek. "You have a cut here." He touched it gently.

"Yes," she murmured, wincing a little. "I also have a bump where he knocked me unconscious."

Bringing his hand up, Nicholas gently pressed it to the back of her head. She hissed in pain when he touched her matted hair.

"I am going to kill him," he declared.

But before he could turn around, Penelope surprised him by wrapping her arms around his waist. "Don't leave me," she pleaded.

In response, he pulled her tightly against him and rested his chin on the top of her head. "Never, my dear, sweet Penelope."

She sighed, and his heart leapt from his chest. It was over. Penelope was safe and back in his arms.

The loud clearing of a throat came from next to them. Nicholas reluctantly turned his head to see who dared interrupt this moment. It was Baldwin. Of course, it was that scoundrel.

"Cousin!" Penelope exclaimed as she stepped out of his embrace and into her cousin's. "What are you doing here?"

Baldwin gave him a smug smile. "His grace asked for my assistance in rescuing you."

"I did not!" he declared. "I specifically forbade him to come."

"I recall it differently," Baldwin joked, but the humor fell from his face when he looked at Penelope's injuries. "We need to get you to a doctor."

Penelope waved a hand dismissively in front of her. "I don't need a doctor, but I would welcome a warm bath."

A cocking of a pistol came from behind them as Everett warned Mr. Pratt in a steely voice, "I wouldn't move, if I were you."

"Everett," Penelope acknowledged him gratefully. "Thank you for coming to my rescue as well."

He tipped his head at her. "I wouldn't have missed it."

Baldwin looked over at Mr. Pratt and asked, "What do we do with him?"

"Besides abducting me to gain access to my company," Penelope shared, "he was also attempting to hide the fact that the Foster Company has been importing slaves to a British colony."

Nicholas did not think that Mr. Pratt could have sunk any lower for abducting a woman, but he was wrong. He also condemned Africans to a life of a hard, miserable existence.

"As much as I would love to see Mr. Pratt hang for his crimes, he most likely would only be issued a fine for breaking the law." He hesitated, before correcting, "Actually, your company would be issued the fine for importing slaves, not Mr. Pratt."

She pursed her lips together. "Will nothing happen to him for everything that he has done to my father's company? To me?"

Seeing the sadness mar her features was Nicholas' undoing. He crouched down next to Mr. Pratt. "If I ever see you again," he threatened in a hushed voice, "I will ruin you. I will take everything you hold dear and cause it to crumble right before your eyes." He patted his shoulder before adding, "And then I will kill you. In the slowest, most excruciating way possible."

Nicholas rose and tugged down on his jacket. "Do I make myself clear, Mr. Pratt?"

Mr. Pratt nodded with fear in his eyes.

"Good." Holding out his hand to Penelope, he asked, "Should we depart for home?"

"Not yet," Baldwin declared, storming past him. He grabbed Mr. Pratt's shirt, yanked him up and knocked him unconscious in one blow. He stood and nodded in satisfaction. "Now I am ready."

Nicholas lifted his brow at the viscount. "That was nicely done."

"You sound surprised," Baldwin huffed.

With Penelope's hand tucked securely into his, Nicholas felt relieved enough to tease Baldwin. "I have been on the receiving end of your blows, and I hardly felt them. It was like a puff of air being directed at me."

Everett let out a bark of laughter as he tucked the pistol back into the waistband of his trousers. "You two are idiots. Entertaining idiots, though."

"I will need to thank Lord Misgrove for allowing us to borrow his dueling pistols," Nicholas commented as he led Penelope to his horse. He reached for the reins, and informed his ward, "I hope you don't mind too terribly, but you and I will be riding together for the journey home."

Her lips parted, and he leaned in to hear what she was about to say. Annoyingly, Baldwin's voice spoke over her. "Absolutely not. It is completely improper for you two to share a horse." He stalked over to them. "My cousin will ride with me."

Nicholas gave him a look of disbelief. "There is nothing proper about this whole situation. She will ride with me."

"Let's ask Penelope," Baldwin suggested, turning to face her.

Penelope's eyes darted between them, and a small smile played on her lips. She found this situation humorous, he realized.

"I would prefer to ride with Nicholas," she answered in a calm voice.

Not giving her a moment to change her mind, he placed his hands on her hips and lifted her onto his saddle. He mounted and gave the viscount a mock salute. "Thank you for your assistance, but I have it from here."

He kicked his horse into a run, knowing the others would eventually catch up to him. Penelope leaned back and rested her head against his chest. A feeling of contentment entered his heart.

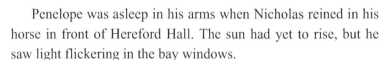

Penelope was asleep in his arms when Nicholas reined in his horse in front of Hereford Hall. The sun had yet to rise, but he saw light flickering in the bay windows.

He didn't want this moment to end, but he needed to get Penelope's wounds tended to. He kissed the top of her head, and she responded by snuggling closer to him. He could get used to that.

"We're home," he informed her.

She lifted her head off his chest, and he immediately regretted his actions. She looked up at him, her eyes heavy with sleep. "I had the most horrific dream," she said in a teasing voice. "I was abducted and was on my way to Gretna Green."

He chuckled at her attempt at humor. "It's a good thing I was there to rescue you."

"It truly was," she replied quickly, her piercing eyes holding him captive. "You were my hero."

A footman exited the main entrance and rushed down the stairs. "My apologies for taking so long, your grace."

"No harm done," he replied, reluctantly tearing his gaze away from Penelope.

He dismounted and reached back up to assist his ward as she dismounted. Once her feet touched the ground, she swayed, and he immediately scooped her back up into his arms.

"My legs must have fallen asleep from the long ride home," she explained, "but if you give me a moment, then I can walk in."

"No need."

He anticipated that she would fight him, but she just wrapped her arms around his neck as he carried her into the entrance hall.

"Hawkins!"

His butler came out of one of the side rooms. "Welcome home, your grace. We have been most worried about you and Miss Foster."

"Did my mother inform you of the situation?"

"She did."

"Good," he declared. "Send a coach to collect Dr. Barnes." He started walking towards the stairs. "Is Miss Foster's lady's maid awake?"

"Yes, she is."

Nicholas bobbed his head in approval. "Excellent. Please see that she prepares a warm bath for Miss Foster immediately."

His mother's excited voice shouted down from the top of the stairs. "You found her!" Her smile dimmed as she watched him rush up the stairs. "Dear child, you are injured."

"The injuries look worse than they are," Penelope said, tightening her hold around his neck.

Nicholas walked down the hall towards his ward's bedchamber. His mother opened the door, and he laid her down on the large four poster bed. Once she was out of his arms, he gently brushed the hair off her cheek and asked, "Can I get you anything?"

"Water, please?" she asked in a raspy voice.

"That's an easy enough request. I shall be right back." Nicholas turned and saw his mother was still by the door. "Would you mind staying with Penelope for a moment?"

"Of course," she said, offering him a tentative smile, "but may I speak with you in the hall first."

Before he followed his mother, he reached for Penelope's hand and squeezed it. "I'll be back shortly."

"Thank you," came her tired response.

Nicholas wondered what his mother wanted to speak to him about, especially at a time like this. To his surprise, his usually calm and collected mother was pacing the floor in an agitated state. "Whatever is the matter?"

She stopped pacing and stepped closer to him, keeping her voice low. "After you left, I overheard Lady Tanner telling a group of busy-bodies that Penelope had fled to Gretna Green with Mr. Pratt."

"How did she know that?"

The duchess threw up her hands. "I don't know. That doesn't matter. Penelope is ruined."

His mind played through various scenarios on how to save his charge from ruination before he focused on the ideal scenario. "Not if we marry," he declared. "We will post the banns today and marry as quickly as possible. Once the ton hears of our engagement, then they will assume Lady Tanner was lying."

"That could work. Did she accept your proposal last night?"

He winced. "We were interrupted."

His mother held her hand out towards the door. "Now's your chance," she encouraged. "I will go get her some water while you offer for her."

"I can't do it now," he huffed. "She is in no position to receive an offer."

The duchess grabbed his sleeve and pushed him into the room. "Good luck," she whispered as she closed the door.

Penelope was sitting up in bed, resting her back against the wall. She gave him a weak smile.

"My mother is getting you a glass of water," he said lamely as he approached her.

"That's most kind of her," Penelope replied, adjusting the sleeve of her soiled white gown

Nicholas went and sat down next to her on the bed, taking a moment to wipe his clammy hands on his trousers. This was ridiculous. Why did the thought of proposing to Penelope cause his heart to beat rapidly in his chest? Could she hear how nervous he was? He had been in many more stressful situations than this. But he couldn't seem to think of one at the moment.

He decided just to tell her the truth and be done with it.

"Lady Tanner somehow discovered that you had left with Mr. Pratt and—"

"I did not leave with him willingly," she interrupted.

"I know, but the ton does not care," he responded in a sympathetic tone. "In order to save your reputation, we must wed. *Immediately.*"

Her lips pressed into a tight white line, and she just stared at him.

Poor Penelope. She must still be in shock. Perhaps she didn't understand the magnitude of the situation, he thought, as he ran his hand through his hair.

"When I say 'immediately', I mean, we will post the banns and marry in three weeks' time at St. George's."

Her frown intensified, and she continued her unrelenting stare. Her words started off reluctant. "If I understand this correctly," she paused, "you are only marrying me to save my reputation."

Finally, she understood. He was doing this for her. "Yes," he said, louder than he had intended. He smiled at her. "Also, my mother wants you for a daughter-in-law." That should make her happy!

The line between her brows appeared again. "No."

"Pardon?"

"My answer is no," she asserted.

He jumped up from the bed in surprise. "You are rejecting my offer?" he exclaimed.

Penelope winced. Then her face changed, her eyes grew determined and her chin rose firmly. "I am."

Turning his back towards her, Nicholas brought his hands up to his head. He had wrongly assumed that she had feelings for him. It mattered not. Penelope had to marry him. He would convince her to fall in love with him, and they would live happily ever after. He was sure of it.

Nicholas spun back around. "I wrongly gave you the impression you had a choice in the matter," he declared, ignoring her gasp of outrage. "The banns will be posted today, and we will be wed."

Her eyes were sparking with anger. "We had a deal…"

He spoke over her. "The deal is off. I am your guardian, and I know what is best for you."

A knock came at the door before Penelope's lady's maid opened the door and announced, "The water is ready, Miss."

Penelope's anger melted as she turned her gaze towards the young maid. "Thank you, Claire. I will be in shortly."

The maid nodded and disappeared back into the hall.

Nicholas walked towards the door and placed his hand on the handle. "This is for the best, you'll see."

Rather than shout at him, her expression softened. "Thank you for rescuing me from Mr. Pratt. I can never repay you." Her words were spoken with tenderness, but it almost sounded like she was saying goodbye. Which was ridiculous. Soon they would be wed, and they would be together always.

He gave her a heartfelt smile. "I would do anything for you, Penelope."

"I know."

"Do you need assistance to your bath?"

She shook her head. "I need some privacy first," she said, lowering her gaze.

"I understand."

Nicholas left the room and closed the door behind him. After Penelope had a long soak and was rested up, she would come to see reason. Marrying him was her only option.

🦋 17 🦋

PENELOPE HAD ANTICIPATED THAT NICHOLAS MIGHT BETRAY HER. After all, she was just the duke's ward. His property. She had no legal rights, and he could make her do anything, including marry him.

The sun was rising as she raced across the south end of the duke's property. She was running towards a small gap in between the rickety fence near the edge of the woods. When she first arrived at Hereford Hall, she had scouted out the property and found multiple ways to escape detection. One never goes into a situation unprepared, she reminded herself.

In between her mattress and frame, she had kept a small reticule with enough money to travel to Miss Bell's Finishing School for Young Ladies. She had no doubt that Miss Bell would assist her, at least until she found employment as a governess or companion.

Penelope slipped through the fence and stopped. She turned back and took a final look at Hereford Hall. When Nicholas had first told her that they were to be wed, she was ecstatic, at least until she saw the expression on his face. He was grimacing during the proposal. Technically, it wasn't even a proposal. It was an order.

Penelope swiped at a tear trailing down her cheek. She loved him, but he didn't love her. He was marrying her only to save her reputation. He was duty-bound to protect her as her guardian. She knew he cared for her, but that was not enough. She would only marry for love.

Strengthening her resolve, she ran towards town and didn't stop until she arrived at the pavement. Women dressed in drab servant's clothing were holding baskets and rushing along, mindful to avoid eye contact with her.

She caught a few women staring at her dress, and she knew they were trying to piece together why she was on the street. Perhaps they spotted the dirt or blood still on her face? Now she regretted that she didn't wait to escape until after a bath and a change of clothes.

Penelope knew her cousin lived at Albany's. Her plan was to wait outside until he left for the day. Then he could help her secure a ride on a mail coach out of town. It seemed like a perfectly acceptable plan when she first came up with it, but that was before she realized she was too weak to walk that far. It was all the way across town, and her legs felt like they were going to give out on her any minute. To make matters worse, she had a throbbing headache that only got worse with each step.

She sat down on the steps of a townhouse and pressed her forehead to the cold iron fence. At least that provided her with some relief. What was she going to do? No hackneys operated at this early hour, and she couldn't very well sit on the pavement all day.

A thought came to her. Lord Northampton's townhouse was just a block over. The duchess had pointed it out when they were traveling to the modiste. He would help her. She was sure of it. Mustering up all her strength, she attempted to walk swiftly to

Everett's townhouse, but found herself growing increasingly weak.

When she finally arrived, Penelope walked up the few steps and knocked on the black door. Due to the early hour, she anticipated a long wait but was pleasantly surprised when the door was opened almost immediately.

A tall, balding butler stood in front of her. "Can I help you, Miss?" His words were spoken with caution, but she heard the compassion in it.

"I am here to see Lord Northampton," she announced, hoping she sounded more confident than she felt.

"Milord is not interested in what you are offering." The butler glanced over his shoulder before turning back to her. He lowered his voice. "If you are hungry, then go around back and knock on the servant's entrance. I will see that the cook will provide you with some sustenance."

Tears pricked her eyes. This man thought she was a woman of loose morals. Could this day get any worse?

Feeling defeated, she started to turn around when she heard Everett's voice coming from inside the townhouse. "Who is calling at such an early hour?"

"No one worthy of your notice, milord," the butler said as he went to close the door.

Knowing this was her one chance to speak to Everett, she shouted as loud as she could, "Everett! I need your help!"

The butler turned towards her with wide eyes, most likely because she had just spoken his master's given name. But she did not care. She needed Everett's help.

Before she could say another word, Everett was at the door, and his eyes ran down the length of her. His cravat was loosed and hung down his shirt. "What's wrong?"

Penelope let out a sigh of relief as she rested her shoulder against the door jamb. Without any hesitation, Lord

Northampton scooped her up in his arms, brought her into the entry foyer and started shouting orders at his butler.

"Send for a doctor and inform Mrs. Hycliff that I need two maids to assist Miss Foster." He turned his attention back to her. "Does Nicholas know you are here?"

She shook her head.

"May I ask why?"

She swallowed slowly. "Someone found out that I left with Mr. Pratt, and I am ruined unless I marry Nicholas."

He looked perplexed. "Is that a bad thing? I couldn't help but notice that you two are enamored with each other."

The butler cleared his throat. "The guest bedroom on the second level is readied, milord."

"Thank you." Everett carried her up the stairs. "I am confused, Penelope. Why are you running away from Nicholas?"

She felt her lower lip tremble as she explained, "He didn't ask me to marry him. He ordered me to."

Everett let out a groan. "Oh dear," he remarked dryly. "I see the problem."

"You do?"

"Not only am I a handsome lord, I can also be quite astute." He winked at her. "You care for him, but you do not believe he returns your feelings."

Feeling bold, she corrected him. "I love him, but he doesn't love me."

Everett came to a stop outside of an opened door. "You love him," he repeated in confusion. "Then why are you leaving him?"

She lowered her gaze, avoiding his scrutiny. "Nicholas is only marrying me because he feels obligated to protect me. He told me that he never wanted to marry. *Ever.* One day, he will grow to resent me, and I could not bear that."

"People can change," he attempted, but she could hear the frown in his voice.

Not that much, she thought to herself. "I will not ruin Nicholas' chances for happiness by forcing him to marry me."

"What if you are his chance at happiness?"

Penelope brought her gaze up to his. "Why would he love someone like me? I have only ever been just a burden to him."

"Did he say that?" Everett asked through clenched teeth.

She shook her head. "No. He didn't need to."

He muttered something under his breath, but she couldn't quite make it out. "Pardon?" she asked.

Everett sighed. "You look a fright. You need to take a bath, and your wounds need to be tended to by a doctor. Furthermore, Nicholas needs to be informed that you are safe."

"No, no, no..." she argued, struggling to get out of his arms. "Please don't tell him I am here. I just need your help to get to my cousin's townhouse at Albany's."

"Then what?" he asked, tightening his hold on her and walking her into the guest bedroom.

Penelope stopped struggling. It was futile to resist Everett's firm grip. "I just have to stay hidden until I turn twenty-one. After that, I will receive my inheritance," she explained.

"I see," he replied in a tone that clearly indicated that he did not. He laid her on the bed and sat down next to her. "I will send up a warm bath and some food for you. I promise that I will not alert Nicholas of your location until after the doctor has tended to you and you have rested for a little while."

Penelope gave him a grateful smile. "Thank you," she said, fully intending to sneak out after the doctor called on her.

Everett looked as though he was attempting to sort out a puzzle in his head. "I have seen the way Nicholas looks at you. I truly believe he has deep feelings for you."

"That was my greatest wish," she breathed. Her eyes grew heavy, knowing she was safe here... at least for a short time.

Everett pulled the covers over her. "I can see how tired you are. Why don't you rest, and we will discuss this more later?"

"Thank you," she murmured before drifting off.

❧ 18 ❧

"YOU LOST HER AGAIN!" BALDWIN EXCLAIMED, STORMING INTO the office.

Nicholas brought his drink up to his lips as he corrected the viscount, "I did not lose her. She ran away." He tossed back his drink and placed the glass onto the drink cart.

A smirk came to Baldwin's lips. "Frankly, it was only a matter of time. I am glad that my cousin finally came to her senses before she was shackled to you."

He clenched his jaw, reconsidering his initial thought that Lord Mountgarret might prove useful. He was wrong, and now he was back to wanting to flog him. "I was hoping she had made contact with you."

"No. I had barely arrived home when your footmen pounded on my door looking for Penelope."

Nicholas dropped onto an upholstered settee and sighed. "Why would she run?"

Baldwin walked over, unbuttoned his jacket, and sat across from him. "How do you know she wasn't abducted again?"

Nicholas grimaced as he reluctantly admitted, "One of my

maids saw Penelope running across the back lawn and disappearing into a wooded section near the back of my property. She immediately reported it to Hawkins. However, by the time he sent footmen out to search for her, they only saw the hole in the fence that she escaped through and small footprints leading towards town."

"Why aren't you out looking for her?"

"I was, in fact, for hours. I was roaming the streets looking for her, and I only just got back." He rubbed his eyes. "I already contacted the Bow Street Runners and every available man is searching for Penelope. I even offered a reward of £10,000 for her safe return."

"I am still at a loss as to why my cousin would run from you," Baldwin said. "She seemed to genuinely care for you."

"I thought so as well, but I was wrong," Nicholas huffed.

The politeness left Baldwin's tone as he asked in an accusing tone, "What did you do?"

"Nothing!" he exclaimed. "I informed her that we needed to be wed to save her reputation."

Baldwin jumped up from his seat. "Pardon?"

"Somehow society's busy body discovered that Penelope left with Mr. Pratt. If we posted the banns today, then all the rumors would be laid to rest as idle gossip."

"Poor Penelope," the viscount sighed, returning to his seat. "Did she see the validity of your recommendation?"

"No," he hesitated, "but she would have eventually come around."

Lord Northampton's voice spoke up from the doorway. "You are horrible at reading women, your grace."

"Where have you been? I sent over a missive that I needed to see you right away," Nicholas asked in annoyance. "That was hours ago."

Walking further into the room, his friend scowled at him.

That's odd, Nicholas thought.

"I received the missive, but I disregarded it. I was too busy tending to Penelope."

Nicholas shot to his feet and advanced towards Everett. "Why do you have my ward?"

"She showed up on my doorstep, looking disheveled and in bad shape," Everett explained. "I ordered a bath for her, contacted the doctor, and ensured she was resting before I came to inform you of her location."

"You had no right to keep Penelope away from me! I have been worried sick!" he exclaimed.

"Good!" Everett shouted. "It's no less than you deserve."

Nicholas' lips parted in surprise. His friend had never been so forceful with him.

"Why do you say that?" he asked through clenched teeth.

Ignoring his question, Everett walked across the room, grabbed the decanter and popped off the top. "I have stood by, observing you and Penelope, and I had hoped that along the way you would have figured out how much she meant to you." He poured himself a drink then put the top back on the decanter. "Instead, you managed to botch up the simplest task."

"And that would be?"

Everett savored his drink before he lowered his glass and answered, "The proposal."

Nicholas rubbed the back of his neck, feeling slightly guilty. "What did she tell you?"

"Let's start with how she informed me that you ordered her to marry you, and when she objected, you told her she had no choice," Everett shared.

Baldwin rose, his face red, his expression murderous. "You promised Penelope that she was allowed to pick her own suitor."

Nicholas dropped his hand as he attempted to explain, "I did, originally. However, that was before her reputation was in tatters. If we don't wed, then she will always be gossiped about." His eyes darted between the two men. "I am doing this to protect Penelope."

Lowering his glass to the drink cart, Everett muttered, "He's hopeless." He turned towards Nicholas with a frown. "You only want to marry Penelope because you wish to protect her. That is the only reason?"

"It is not the only reason," Nicholas started. "I care for the girl."

"I daresay you have greater feelings for Penelope than you are admitting," Baldwin observed. "What I want to know is why?"

Nicholas was done with this ridiculous line of questioning. Penelope was his ward, and he had a right to bring her home. Walking over to his desk, he informed Everett, "I will send over a coach to retrieve Pene…"

"You won't find her," Everett declared, cutting him off. "I should have taken her the first time you offered her up to me."

"Unbelievable!" Baldwin shouted. "You were trying to give away my cousin?"

Nicholas pressed his lips together. "At first, I was hesitant to be guardian to Penelope, but that quickly changed."

Everett placed his palms down on the desk and leaned in, "Why did it change?"

"We became friends," he replied vaguely.

"Just friends?" Everett pressed.

Nicholas narrowed his eyes. "What exactly do you want from me? Just say it and be done with it."

Pushing off from the desk, Everett shook his head in disappointment. "You don't deserve her, you know."

"Don't you think I know that?" Nicholas shouted. "Penelope is better than me in every possible way. Her smile can light up any room. Her blue eyes remind me of the ocean, and when I stare deep into them, I feel at home." He started pacing. "When she speaks to me, she has the ability to wipe away all my fears, my weaknesses."

He stopped pacing and closed his eyes, ignoring the deafening silence of the room. He loved Penelope. But, in his heart, he knew he wasn't good enough for her.

"Why didn't you say those words in the proposal?" Baldwin teased. "I am sure my cousin would have much rather heard those words than orders to marry you."

Nicholas felt dejected. "Don't you see? I will never be good enough for her."

Everett walked over to him and placed his hand on his shoulder. "You're wrong. Penelope is your love match, in every sense of the word."

"She may be mine, but I will never be hers," he said, slumping his shoulder.

The corners of Everett's mouth twitched. "I was concerned that Penelope might try to escape again so I had the doctor put some laudanum in her tea." He removed his hand from his shoulder. "Before she fell into a deep sleep, she spent a good thirty minutes telling me all the reasons she loves you."

Hope blossomed in Nicholas' heart. "Do you think she truly meant it?"

"I do, every word. Penelope ran away from you, because she is in love with you," Everett informed him.

Now he was baffled. "Then why would she run from me? That doesn't make a lot of sense."

"Women are a tricky lot. They say one thing, but they mean another." Everett grinned. "Penelope was insistent that you would grow to resent her because you never wanted to marry in the first place."

It was starting to make sense to him. "That's true. I never intended to marry," Nicholas paused, "until I fell in love with her." It felt so good to say those words out loud. "I love Penelope."

Everett looked up at the ceiling and shouted, "Hallelujah! You can be taught."

"It was painful though," Baldwin stated. "I didn't think he would ever figure it out."

Turning to look at the viscount, Everett nodded in agreement. "It still amazes me that Nicholas was able to beat the French so soundly."

"Beating the French was always easy," Nicholas remarked, not minding the joking at his expense. "I would much rather be outnumbered and outgunned against the enemy than attempt to understand the intricacies of women."

The humor dropped from his expression as he asked his next question with dread. "Do you think I'm too late?"

Everett shook his head. "Not at all. But I would practice your proposal on the way over to my townhouse. Your first attempt was awful, if you can even call it an attempt," he joked.

Nicholas knew he had one shot at making this right with Penelope. He couldn't lose her. Knowing what he needed to do, he walked over to Baldwin and asked, "I may be Penelope's guardian, but you are her relation." He met his gaze, unwavering. "I would like to ask your permission to offer for Penelope."

Baldwin watched him for a moment before extending his hand towards him. "You have my permission, but the choice is my cousin's, and hers alone."

He shook the viscount's hand. "If Penelope will have me, I will treat her with the love and respect she deserves. I promise."

Everett chuckled behind him. "I am not fully convinced you won't botch up the proposal again, but this step was promising."

As he dropped Baldwin's hand, he could see him trying to stifle a laugh. These men were bloody fools. He didn't have time for this. He needed to convince Penelope to marry him. And that might take a long, long time.

Penelope's eyelids felt heavy as she attempted to open them. The thought that she should return to blissful sleep floated in her mind, but she knew she couldn't succumb to it. She had rested long enough. It was time for her to journey on. If Nicholas found her, then he would never let her go. Why did that thought excite and terrify her at the same time?

She pried her eyes open and noticed that the room was bathed in light. How long had she been asleep? She turned her head on her pillow, and her heart stopped. Nicholas was sitting next to the bed, his arms crossed over his chest, and his head was drooping forward. He was asleep.

Moving slowly, Penelope quietly pushed the sheets off her and shifted so her feet were hanging off the bed. She glanced down at her clothing and realized that she was wearing a white nightgown. Now how was she going to escape? She couldn't very well wander the streets in a nightgown.

Her eyes scanned the room, but there was no sign of her white gown. Perhaps she could borrow a maid's uniform for a few hours. It wasn't her best plan, but she didn't have a lot of options.

Nicholas' voice broke through her musings, startling her. "If you are attempting to formulate a plan to escape from me, then you should stop. I have no intention of ever letting you out of my sight again."

If he thought she would give up without a fight, then he was wrong. Penelope met his gaze, defiantly. "I will not marry you," she stated in a firm tone. "You left me no choice but to run away."

"Did I now?" His lips quirked into a crooked smile, making

her decisively more irritated at him. "That was your only option?"

Her eyes took in his haggard appearance. His hair was tousled, he wasn't wearing a cravat or a jacket, and she noticed the dark stubble that ran along his jawline. Even now, she thought he was the most handsome man she had ever seen. He had only grown more attractive in her eyes as she had gotten to know him.

"It was," she asserted.

Nicholas placed his hands on the chair's arms, picking it up and moving it closer to her. Once he was situated, he brought his gaze up to hers and traces of deep thinking appeared on his brow. His usual confidence was stripped away, and he appeared vulnerable.

"Penelope…" His voice stopped, and he shifted his gaze to over her shoulder.

"What is it?" she asked, curious about what could make this strong man so nervous.

He brought his gaze back to her as he reached for her hands in her lap. "I have commanded over a hundred men, fought in numerous battles at sea, dealt with death and heartache, and…" he hesitated, looking down at their entwined hands, "I have never been more scared than I was when you were abducted."

"Oh," she murmured, attempting to pull back her hands.

Refusing to let her go, he pressed, "Do you want to know why?"

"I know why," she answered in an exasperated fashion. "As my guardian, you are obligated to protect me."

"That's part of it, but mostly it was because I am in love with you."

His words were spoken so smoothly that she feared she misheard him. "Pardon?"

Nicholas leaned closer to her. "I don't know when I started to fall in love with you, but I suspect it was at our first meeting.

Even with that ridiculous orange dress and those obnoxiously large spectacles, you were breathtaking, and every day, you have grown more beautiful to me."

Penelope felt herself blushing as he rose and sat down next to her on the bed. His brown eyes were imploring. "You are headstrong, stubborn, irrational, a rule breaker..."

She cut him off. "Are you attempting to compliment me or insult me?"

Bringing his hand up, he tucked a piece of her errant hair behind her ear. "Compliment you, I assure you. You are all those things, and yet, you are also kind, compassionate and forgiving," he replied. "No one has ever challenged me as you have. It is petrifying and exhilarating at the same time."

Penelope was unable to formulate a response as Nicholas' hand tenderly traced her cheekbone.

His eyes darted down to her lips, before slowly bringing his gaze back up. "When I am awake, I long to be near you, and when I close my eyes at night, I dream of you."

She finally found the courage to ask, "Do you truly mean it?"

"Which part?" His finger started trailing along her bottom lip.

"All of it."

His eyes lit up with merriment. "Yes, I mean every single word."

"Oh," she breathed.

Encompassing both of her hands, Nicholas slipped off the bed and knelt before her. "I want to marry you, not just to protect you, but because I love you," he said. "You have reminded me to laugh, taught me how to forgive, and," he stopped, and brought her hands up to his lips and kissed them, "you have become my saving grace."

Tears came to her eyes, but she didn't move to wipe them away. These were happy tears. "Did you ask me to marry you or did you just issue another order?" she asked cheekily.

He grinned. "Miss Penelope Foster, will you do me the honor of becoming my wife?"

She pulled her hands back to cover the squeal that came from her lips. "Yes," she exclaimed, jumping into his awaiting arms.

Nicholas let out a hearty laugh as they embraced. After a moment, he scooped her up in his arms and sat down on the bed, placing her in his lap.

"I take it that this proposal was more to your liking," he teased.

She giggled. "Your first attempt was awful."

"I was worried you would say no," he admitted, shrugging.

Tentatively, Penelope brought her fingers up to run it along his strong jawline, fascinated by the feeling of the dark stubble growing there. "My heart chose you a long time ago," she revealed. "I love you."

"Then why did you leave me?"

"You told me that you never wanted to marry, and I was afraid…" She stopped and dropped her hand.

"Afraid of what?" he pressed gently.

She lowered her voice. "I was afraid that you would resent me for forcing you into a marriage that you didn't want."

Nicholas brought his hands up and cupped her cheeks, forcing her to look at him. "It is true that the thought of marriage petrified me, but that was before I met you." He stared deep into her eyes. "Now when I think about my future, it is filled with joy and laughter. All because of you."

Feeling an exorbitant amount of love, she leaned forward and pressed her lips tightly against his. She felt and heard him murmur her name against her closed lips. Leaning back, she asked, "Did I do something wrong?"

The corner of his mouth lifted, and he edged closer. "Anytime I feel your lips on mine is perfect. But perhaps I can demonstrate another way."

Penelope nodded, unsure of his intent. He lowered his head

to brush his lips against hers, causing tingles to course throughout her body. Just when she thought it couldn't get any better, he deepened the kiss, and she found herself melting into his arms.

Her hands slid around his neck, and she wove her fingers through his hair. For her first kissing experience, this was going fantastically well, she thought, as a slight moan escaped from the back of her throat.

Nicholas pulled her tighter against him, and his lips became more demanding. But she had no complaints. If anything, she never wanted him to stop.

A loud clearing of a throat came from the door. "Your time is up, your grace," Everett declared.

"If we ignore him, will he go away?" Penelope asked, her lips brushing against his.

Nicholas let out a deep chuckle. "There is only one way to find out," he answered, pressing his lips to hers.

Everett cleared his throat again, but this time he had stepped further into the room. "Nicholas," he warned. "Don't make me call for Baldwin."

Nicholas let out a groan as he leaned back. "Why did you have to bring him up?"

It was Everett's turn to laugh. "I knew it would kill the mood for you."

Penelope started to move off his lap, but Nicholas held her tight against him. "Where do you think you are going?"

She smiled, enjoying this playful side of Nicholas. "I can't very well stay in your lap all day."

"I don't see a problem with that," he quipped.

The door opened, and Baldwin stepped into the room. His eyes narrowed, and he opened his mouth, no doubt to give them a tongue lashing, but then closed it. He shut the door and then advanced towards them. "Cousin," he said sharply.

Penelope quickly moved off Nicholas' lap. "Baldwin. I can explain."

To her surprise, her cousin's face broke out into a huge smile. "I take it that you and his grace are engaged." He embraced her. "I am happy for you."

He must be mocking her, she thought. "Truly?"

"His grace and I have put our differences aside," Baldwin paused, before adding, "at least some of them. He even asked my permission to offer for you."

Penelope glanced between them in confusion. "How long was I asleep?"

Nicholas rose from the bed and slid an arm around her waist. "I am relieved that you agreed to marry me, because the banns were posted this morning."

"Does this mean we have to wait three weeks to get married?" Penelope asked with a slight pout of her lip.

"No," Nicholas said.

"Yes," Baldwin replied, in unison.

Everett was the voice of reason. "The duchess would be furious if you two were married by special license, thus denying her an opportunity to plan a wedding luncheon."

"Good point," she agreed.

Nicholas turned her in his arms to face him and placed his other arm around her waist. "That means I will have three weeks to properly court you."

Ignoring the groans of the other men in the room, Penelope gave her betrothed a coy smile. "I can't wait."

EPILOGUE

Penelope was reviewing the ledgers from her company when Nicholas slipped his arm around her shoulders. He leaned closer and kissed her ear, making it immensely more difficult to focus.

"I thought you had work to do," she stated breathlessly as he lowered his lips to her neck.

"I find it hard to concentrate when you are looking so incredibly beautiful today," he replied between kisses.

"You were the one that moved my writing desk into your study so we could be together while we worked."

"I do so love being close to you," he said flirtatiously.

A smile came to her lips. "We are leaving for our wedding tour tomorrow, and you informed me at breakfast that you would be incredibly busy today."

He brought his lips back up to her ear, nibbling on it. "I did. But I would much rather spend time with my wife."

My wife. Penelope would never tire of Nicholas saying that. He had been true to his word and courted her intently for three weeks before they wed at St. George's. Between rides in the morning and social events in the evening, they had spent almost every waking moment together. It was perfect.

A week after the banns had been posted, they celebrated with their engagement ball, which originally was intended as her coming-out ball. Penelope didn't mind since she was able to dance with her fiancé all night, and her dear friends from Miss Bell's Finishing School attended as well. Furthermore, Nicholas had been right. After the banns were posted, and the ton saw how enamored they were with each other, the story of Mr. Pratt was dismissed as gossip.

"Would you like to continue this in our bedchamber?" Nicholas whispered in her ear.

"You are incorrigible," she teased, turning in his arms. "We already enjoyed a lot of time in our bedchamber this morning."

A boyish grin came to his lips. "Not enough time if you ask me."

She sighed dramatically. "All right. I suppose I could use a break."

As soon as she said those words, Nicholas whooped and scooped her up in his arms, causing her to squeal and laugh at his eagerness. He strode towards the door, determination in his stride.

"Your graces," Mr. Hawkins said respectfully as he appeared at the doorway of the study, blocking their retreat.

Nicholas stopped and declared, "Whatever it is can wait. We are currently occupied."

Hawkins wore a look of mild amusement. "Lord Mountgarret is here to see you."

"Baldwin ruins all the fun," Nicholas expressed through clenched teeth.

Penelope brought her hand up to cover her growing smile. Her husband may claim he could not stand Baldwin, but they had grown closer these pasts few weeks as well.

Nicholas brought his gaze to hers and asked, "You think this is funny?"

"Immensely," she joked.

His lips quirked in the corners, but he managed to maintain a stoic expression fairly successfully. "Tell Mountgarret that we will be with him in thirty minutes... no, forty minutes."

"That will not do," Baldwin proclaimed, appearing next to Hawkins at the door. "After all, I responded to your request that I come to call today."

Penelope laughed when Baldwin walked into the room and dropped down on the sofa, eliciting a low growl from the back of Nicholas' throat.

Nicholas leaned closer to her ear and whispered, "Don't get too comfortable. As soon as your cousin leaves, we will pick up where we left off."

She smiled coyly at him. "I suppose I can wait."

Her husband gently released her from his arms and escorted her to a settee. He waited for her to be seated before he sat down next to her.

"Despite your horrible timing, we are grateful that you came to call," Nicholas said.

Baldwin adjusted his blue riding jacket. "I was surprised to receive your missive this morning, considering you were married yesterday, and you are leaving on your wedding tour tomorrow."

"Yes, well, we have something important that we need to discuss with you," Nicholas stated.

"Which is?" Baldwin asked, glancing between them.

Her husband offered her a private smile before answering him. "We may have started out under bad terms..."

Baldwin spoke over him. "You accused me of nefarious intentions with Penelope." He winked at her, and his words were spoken lightly.

Nicholas chuckled. "True, but ultimately, we both only cared about Penelope's best interest. Which is why I have paid off all your outstanding debts and have hired an architect to begin restoring your estate."

"Absolutely not!" Baldwin turned his gaze towards Penelope. "You promised me that you wouldn't get involved in my affairs."

She nodded. "I did, but Nicholas did not. That was his wedding gift to me, and I thought it was perfect."

Baldwin pursed his lips before saying, "Thank you. I will find a way to pay back every pound."

"You will not," Nicholas stated. "It is a gift, not a loan."

"It's too much," Baldwin replied, shaking his head. "I appreciate your generosity, but I am not a charity case."

Nicholas met his gaze with a forthright expression. "You're right. You are not a charity case. You are family. And family looks out for one another."

After a long moment, Baldwin relented. "Thank you."

Nicholas turned his expectant gaze to her, and she knew it was her turn to surprise her cousin. "My father loved you very much," she started, "and I have no doubt, that if he had lived longer, he would have been very proud of who you have become."

"He was the best of men. At times, he was more of a father to me than my own father. I miss him," Baldwin said in a wistful tone.

"I miss him too," she replied, her voice hitching. "I also know that he would have ensured you were taken care of as well. So, I have decided to give you equal partnership in the Foster Company."

"What?" Baldwin's eyes grew wide. "No, no, no... I cannot accept that. I will not. That is your company."

Penelope smiled fondly at her cousin. "It's our company now."

"I can't let you do this," Baldwin asserted. "This is too much."

"Do you remember when we toured one of my father's

merchant ships when we were younger?" she asked. He nodded, and she continued. "My father put his arms around both of our shoulders and told us that this would belong to us one day."

Baldwin's expression grew sorrowful. "That was just before the accident."

"It was, but I did not forget." Penelope shifted so she sat on the edge of her seat. "I want you to have a chance to marry for love, as I did." She snuck a loving glance over her shoulder at Nicholas. "You now have the freedom to do so."

"Thank you..." Baldwin's voice was choked with emotion. "Thank you to both of you."

Placing her hands in her lap, she replied, "I do have one condition."

"Anything," her cousin said without delay.

Penelope tried not to laugh at his overeager tone. "Both Pratts have a warrant out for their arrests and have disappeared. Our company is in desperate need of new leadership, and I would like us to run it... together."

"Both of us?" he asked. "You want me to be involved in the business?"

"I do," she stated.

A bright smile came to his face. "I think that's brilliant. We'll get to spend more time together."

Nicholas reached for her hand in her lap. "Due to my suspicions about you, I had the Bow Street Runners investigate you, and I learned that you have a keen sense when it comes to business."

Baldwin held up his hands in front of him. "That's not true. As you are aware, I am heavily in debt... was heavily in debt," he corrected.

"You inherited almost all of your debt from your father, and slowly, through wise investment choices, you've chipped away at that debt," Nicholas praised. "I have no doubt that you would have gotten yourself out of that hole eventually. I am confident that you will do great things at the Foster Company."

Baldwin wiped his hand over his mouth as he regarded Nicholas. "Thank you for your encouraging words. I am still amazed at how much my life has changed since I walked through your doors."

Nicholas grew serious. "I was wrong about you, and I apologize. When Penelope's life was in danger, you put our differences aside and helped me rescue her. That is a debt that I can never repay."

"You're wrong. You paid that debt by loving my cousin," Baldwin replied. "I can see the joy in her eyes, and that's all that I have ever wanted for her."

Penelope sat back and leaned into her husband. Her heart was so full. She had gotten her wish. She had married for love, and it was better than she had ever imagined. For with Nicholas by her side, she would never be alone or forgotten again.

REGENCY BRIDES: A PROMISE OF LOVE SERIES

Lady Madalene Ramsbury has been summoned home from Miss Bell's Finishing School to some unfortunate news. In three weeks, she is to be married to a man she's never met. Rather than

face a life she does not want; she flees from her own engagement party and elicits help from a most unlikely source.

Society's golden boy, Everett, the Marquess of Northampton, was outraged when a young woman suddenly appeared in his curricle. Was she attempting to trap him into an unwanted marriage? It would be just like some overzealous mother to put her up to such a ploy. However, it doesn't take long for him to discover that Madalene is unlike any woman he has ever known.

With her reputation in shambles, Lady Madalene and Everett hatch a plan to solve both of their problems, a fake engagement. But as they spend time together, they realize more is on the line than just a blossoming friendship. And with danger ever present from her jilted suitor, Everett and Madalene find themselves relying on one another in ways they'd never imagined... but can they trust each other with their hearts?

ABOUT THE AUTHOR

Laura Beers is an award-winning author. She attended Brigham Young University, earning a Bachelor of Science degree in Construction Management. She can't sing, doesn't dance and loves naps.

Besides being a full-time homemaker to her three kids, she loves waterskiing, hiking, and drinking Dr. Pepper. She was born and raised in Southern California, but she now resides in South Carolina.

You can reach her at authorlaurabeers@gmail.com

Made in the USA
Monee, IL
31 January 2023

26823603R00115